MURDER
with a *Twist*

TRACY KIELY

MURDER
with a *Twist*

MIDNIGHT INK
WOODBURY, MINNESOTA

FIRST EDITION
First Printing, 2015

Book design and format by Donna Burch-Brown
Cover design by Kevin R. Brown
Cover illustration: Kim Johnson/Lindgren & Smith
Editing by Connie Hill

Midnight Ink, an imprint of Llewellyn Worldwide Ltd.

Library of Congress Cataloging-in-Publication Data

Kiely, Tracy.
  Murder with a twist / Tracy Kiely. — First edition.
    pages ;   cm. — (A Nic & Nigel mystery ; #1)
  Summary: "Nic and Nigel Martini are visiting New York to attend a cousin's birthday gala, but when the birthday girl's gold-digging cad of a husband goes missing, the social event of the season may turn into a story for the scandal sheets. Nigel's condescending aunt begs Nic to find sleazy Leo, despite the fact that it would be better for everyone if he just stayed lost. Trailing a married bachelor with a penchant for trouble can be downright deadly. Assisted by Nigel and their bull mastiff, Nic must tangle with her old underworld connections if she hopes to hunt down the killer"—Publisher.
  ISBN 978-0-7387-4372-1 (softcover)
  I. Title.
  PS3611.I4453M9   2015
  813'.6—dc23   2014042211

Midnight Ink
Llewellyn Worldwide Ltd.
2143 Wooddale Drive
Woodbury, MN 55125-2989
www.midnightinkbooks.com
Printed in the United States of America

This book is dedicated, with love,
to Ann Mahoney, with whom I saw *The Thin Man*
for the very first time. It was one of many great days
I spent with you. I love you very much!

ACKNOWLEDGMENTS

I have so many people I need to thank. My agent, Barbara Poelle, for believing in me and always making me laugh. My editor, Terri Bischoff, for taking a chance on me. For Barbara Kiely, Bridget Kiely, MaryAnn Kingsley, Terri Mullen-Sweeney, Joelle Charbonneau, Sophie Littlefield, and the Bunco Ladies for all your continued and much-needed support. And, of course, for my wonderful family— my husband, Matt, and our amazing children, Jack, Elizabeth, and Pat. Thanks so much for putting up with my crazy. I love you!

ONE

I WAS LEANING AGAINST the bar in a hotel on 57th Street, waiting for Nigel to finish his Christmas shopping, when a woman got up from a table and came over. She was blonde and slim, and whether you looked at her face or at her body clad in a silky blue dress, the result was a credit to money and good genes.

"Are you Nicole Martini?" she asked.

"That's me," I answered.

"I'm Daphne Beasley. I'm Nigel's cousin."

"Oh, of course," I said, as we leaned in to give each other the polite hugs expected between casual female acquaintances. "I didn't recognize you at first. How have you been?"

"Good, thanks. I graduated from law school last year, and started at my dad's firm. I know it looks like nepotism—probably because it is—but I've been busting my tail off to quiet the skeptics. So far, it seems to be working."

"Congratulations."

"Thanks." With a subtle flick of her bejeweled wrist, she summoned the bartender. "Grey Goose and tonic, Tony," she said to a slight man with dark hair and darker eyes, whose name I hoped rather than assumed was Tony. Turning to me, she added, "Would you like anything?"

"No, thanks. I'm fine," I said, indicating my club soda.

Moments later Tony appeared with her drink. Placing it on a linen napkin, he slid the crystal tumbler toward her and stepped back to wait for her approval. She took a sip and nodded her thanks. I half-expected Tony to click his heels in response. Thankfully, he didn't. "Listen, you used to be a detective, right?" she asked, focusing again on me.

"That's right."

"But you retired?"

"In a manner of speaking. I got shot and then put on desk duty," I answered, glancing down at my leg that still ached from time to time. "The desk and I didn't suit."

"So, do you practice at all anymore?"

"Mainly, I practice not getting shot. Why do you ask?"

"I'm worried about Audrey."

Audrey is another of Nigel's cousins. In a few days she was turning twenty-five. We were in New York for Christmas week to celebrate both her and the baby Jesus's birthday. This being a Martini event, Audrey's milestone got top billing. The associated festivities were expected to be lengthy and expensive. Lengthy and expensive is one of many Martini traditions.

"What's wrong with Audrey?"

"It isn't so much what's wrong with her as it's what's wrong with that horrible husband of hers. Have you met Leo?"

"No, but your mother described him to me once. I believe she used the term 'dirty married bachelor.'"

Daphne produced a grim smile. "Mother does have a way with words, even if they aren't hers, but that's Leo. He looks like one of those Euro-trash models. You know the type; ridiculously slim with slicked-back hair. Wears those stupid suits that look like they shrunk in the wash."

"Sounds charming. Other than his fashion sense, what's the problem?"

She sighed. "The problem is that he's disappeared."

I took a sip of my drink and wondered where the hell Nigel was. "Wouldn't that be a good thing, given the whole dirty married bachelor thing?"

"You'd think so, but Audrey is a mess. For whatever unknown reason, she loves him. If he doesn't show up at her birthday party, she'll be humiliated. She knows what the family thinks of him. Given all that she's been through, I don't know if she could face it."

Audrey's parents died in a plane crash five years ago. David and Rose Martini were extremely wealthy—even by Martini family standards—and Audrey was an only child. She inherited a king's ransom upon their death and, under the terms of her trust fund, was due to inherit even more upon turning twenty-five. A shy and somewhat plain girl, she was forever suspicious that the men in her life were with her for the wrong reasons. Unfortunately, she was usually right.

"You want me to find Leo?" I asked, deciding to cut to the chase.

Daphne produced a grateful smile and nodded. "Well, it's really more Mother's idea than mine, but yes. Could you?"

I shook my head. "I doubt it. After all, I'm retired and haven't worked with the Department since Nigel and I moved out to LA. I wouldn't even know where to begin to look."

"I might be able to help you there," Daphne said. "I have a few leads."

"Then why don't you find him?"

She pulled a face and stared at her glass. Slowly rubbing her index finger along the rim, she said, "I don't think that's such a good idea." Before I could ask why, a loud commotion behind me caught my attention. Glancing up at the enormous expanse of mirror behind the bar, I stared past my own reflection and saw a tall, dark, handsome man being dragged across the room by what appeared to be an enormous mastiff. Three chairs and one barstool went down in their wake. Bar chatter subsided as the patrons quieted to watch the unfolding spectacle. Within seconds both the dog and the man were in front of me. The dog nudged his face into my stomach; the man nudged his face into my neck.

"Hello, darling," he said. The man; not the dog.

"Hello," I replied in kind. "Why do you have a dog with you?"

"He followed me."

"Nigel, he's on a leash. If anything, you're following him. Why do you have a dog with you?"

"The man at the pet store said you wouldn't like the piranha."

"The man at the pet store is wise," I said, tentatively pushing the dog's square head away from my stomach.

"His name is Skippy," Nigel offered.

"I highly doubt that," I said, eyeing the dog.

"Hello, Nigel," Daphne now said. "It's good to see you."

"Daphne! I didn't see you. You look wonderful. How are you?" Nigel replied while trying to stop Skippy from eating the complimentary bar snacks. He failed. Skippy:1; Nigel: 0.

Tony returned and produced an apologetic cough. "I'm sorry, sir, but we don't allow dogs in the bar."

Nigel nodded. "I understand, but he's a Seeing Eye dog. However, he's very modest about it, so please don't say anything to him."

Tony stared at Nigel. "He's a Seeing Eye dog for whom?"

"I'm afraid that's classified," Nigel said. "May I have a scotch and soda, please?"

Tony appeared to debate reiterating his request that Skippy leave. After staring at Skippy's massive fawn-colored head, which was now casually resting atop the glossy marble bar, he decided to let the matter go and went off to get Nigel's drink.

"Same old Nigel," Daphne said with a laugh.

"Well, I should hope so," Nigel replied. "So, how are you?"

"Fine," Daphne replied. "I was just trying to convince your lovely wife here to take on a case for me."

Nigel turned to me and raised an eyebrow. "Easy, darling," I said. "Before you get your hopes up, it's *not* a case of scotch."

TWO

"WHAT KIND OF CASE?" Nigel asked Daphne, ignoring me. Skippy, however, focused his huge brown eyes on me and wagged his tail. It thumped against the bar. I stepped back a few inches to avoid having my leg further maimed.

"I want Nic to help me find Leo," said Daphne. "He's taken off. *Again.* Normally, I wouldn't care, but Audrey will be devastated if he's a no-show for her party."

"What do you mean 'again'?" I asked. "How often does he take off like this?"

"Just about every time a pretty bimbo catches his eye," Daphne replied with a sneer. "Which is, I'm sorry to say, quite often. Normally, I'd pray that this is the time he doesn't come skulking back. However, I want him at that party."

"I see. And do we want the pretty bimbo there as well?" Nigel asked.

"Of course not! Don't get me wrong. I wish Audrey had never met Leo. The man's disgusting. He's nothing but a wolf in cheap clothing." Nigel winced. "I just want Leo there for her party," Daphne continued. "It's hard to explain, but I want him there if for no other reason than to protect Audrey's ego on her birthday. Once the party's over, he can crawl back into whatever hole he slithered out of. Hell, I'll even help him pack."

Nigel's eye twitched. "Stop that!" he begged. "What do you have against metaphors anyway?"

Daphne glanced at Nigel in confusion. Against the general hum of conversation and tinkling glass in the bar, a faint ringtone now sounded. Daphne pulled a phone from her leather clutch, glanced at the screen, and frowned. "I'm sorry, I need to take this. You two are staying here at the hotel, right?"

Nigel and I nodded. "Good. I'll see you later then. Bye!" She blew us what I hoped was meant to be an air kiss and then turned, jamming the phone against her ear. "What did you find out?" I heard her say as she walked away.

I pivoted toward Nigel. "You'd better have gotten me one hell of Christmas present. I have a feeling I'm going to deserve it."

"You already deserve it," he answered. "Do you want a drink?"

"Yes, please," I answered. I caught Tony's eye. In the last ten minutes, I'd acquired a new dog and a lost married bachelor case. It had been a few years since I'd been a detective, but it seemed that this weekend was going to require something stiffer than my usual club soda and lime. Oddly, I was game.

THREE

BACK IN OUR HOTEL room, Nigel was sprawled on the bed. I sat at the dressing table. Skippy was stretched out on the coffee-colored club chair and its corresponding ottoman. He appeared to be sleeping. I didn't ask how Nigel convinced the hotel staff to let Skippy stay with us, nor did I intend to. I suspected it had something to do with one of us having epileptic seizures.

"So what do you want to do?" Nigel asked.

"I'm amenable for repeating what we just did."

"I meant about Leo. But your wish is my command."

I put down my hairbrush. "Do you really think I should find Leo? It sounds as if Audrey would be better off if he stayed lost."

"Agreed. But Audrey has been through a lot, poor kid. And, of course, I only mean 'poor' in the figurative sense."

"Of course," I agreed. I pumped some lotion into the palm of my hand and rubbed it in. "I've never met Leo. Is he really as bad as everyone says?"

Nigel propped himself up on one elbow, affording me a most enjoyable view of his chest. "I guess so. He's your typical good-looking, charming, gold digger who seduces the naïve rich."

"I didn't know there were any of those left in the world."

"Charming gold diggers?"

"Naïve rich."

Nigel affected a demure expression. "Well, no. I guess not," he said, glancing at the crumpled sheets. "Especially not after this afternoon."

FOUR

THAT EVENING, THE THREE of us (Nigel having declared that Skippy was now a member of the family) braved the cold and walked to Nigel's Aunt Olive's for dinner. When we were first married, Nigel argued that I shouldn't refer to her as *his* aunt, insisting that she was as much my aunt now as his. However, I insisted just as vehemently that "for better and for worse, and in sickness and in health" did not include his Aunt Olive.

Walking wasn't our preferred method of travel, but New York cabbies, while generally tolerant souls, apparently draw the line at transporting animals resembling small ponies. Undeterred, Skippy led us with a purposeful stride for the first four blocks until Nigel was forced to concede that perhaps Skippy's calling in life was something other than a Seeing Eye dog. We dutifully backtracked our steps and set out on the correct route.

Nigel's Aunt Olive lives in the Ritz Tower with her husband, Max Beasley. Most consider Max to be the perfect counterpart for

Olive as he is a large, jovial man, and she is not. The Martini family initially resisted their relationship, as Max was an attorney with the firm that handled the family's financial affairs. However, in the end, their love overcame all obstacles. Well, their love and a healthy desire by Olive to finally rid herself of her maiden name.

At the Ritz, the uniformed doorman waved us through the entrance with a respectful flourish, his professional countenance slipping only momentarily at the sight of Skippy. Inside, Nigel and I chatted politely with Frances, the residential concierge, who also pretended that two-hundred-pound monstrosities eagerly trying to climb atop her wooden desk were an everyday occurrence. I tried to imagine an instance in which similar leeway would be given to members of the less fortunate class. Then I tried to imagine Santa Claus.

After polite conversation was duly exchanged on both sides, Frances buzzed us into the elevators. The gilded doors slid quietly together, slowly compressing a vision of her gamely waving a polite goodbye to us.

"So, why are we having dinner with your aunt and uncle again?" I asked, as I simultaneously punched the button for the thirty-fourth floor and tried to block Skippy from punching additional floor buttons with his nose. I failed on the latter. Skippy: 8; Me: 0.

"For the good company, of course."

"Is that a new catering service?"

"No."

"Then try again."

The elevator eased to a stop at the first of Skippy's requested floors (eleven through seventeen). At floor sixteen, Skippy barked happily, startling a bony, anemic woman who promptly yelped and skittered away.

"Don't you find my family endearing?" Nigel asked. "I'm beginning to think that you married me just for my assets."

"I find *you* endearing," I offered. "But you can't expect your assets *not* to play a role in our relationship." I playfully swatted his rear. "Especially when you wear those pants."

"Now I feel faintly dirty."

"You're welcome."

We alighted at the thirty-fourth floor and made our way down the thickly carpeted hallway to Aunt Olive's door. "Whenever your Aunt Olive calls us to her house, I always feel as if I've been summoned to my execution," I said.

Nigel scoffed. "Don't be silly. If she really wanted you dead, she'd hire a hit man. Much neater that way."

"Thank you, dear. That's most reassuring."

We were at their door. Nigel leaned over and kissed me lightly on my mouth. "Don't worry, darling. You're perfectly safe. Besides, I'm pretty sure if she's going to kill anyone, it's going to be Leo."

Nigel gave the door a sharp knock. Within seconds a large, fleshy-faced man wearing an ill-fitting black suit opened it.

Upon seeing me, his expression morphed from one of professional coolness to that of mild distress. It was an expression I'd grown accustomed to seeing on the various faces of the snobbier members of Nigel's family in the years since we'd married. However, the reason I was seeing it now had nothing to do with my family's undistinguished pedigree.

"Dear God," I said. "Joe? Joe Abrams? When did you get out of prison?"

Joe shifted his massive weight uncomfortably, his small eyes darting over his shoulder to where I assumed his new employers sat in happy oblivion regarding their new butler's sordid past.

"I got out for good behavior six months ago," Joe said, his voice low. "I'm rehabilitated now. The court said so."

"Well, that's good enough for me," said Nigel, putting out his hand. "I'm Nigel, by the way. Nic's husband." The two shook hands. "And this is Skippy," Nigel said proudly. Skippy wagged his tail and sniffed Joe's knees.

Joe awkwardly patted Skippy's head. "Nice, Skippy," he finally said.

"So, what were you in for?" Nigel asked in a conspiratorial tone.

"Trafficking stolen property," Joe mumbled after another backward glance.

"Among other lofty pursuits, Joe stole and sold flat-screen TVs," I explained.

Nigel adopted an impressed expression. "And my brilliant wife tracked you down and caught you?"

"It wasn't too hard," I demurred. "Joe's get-a-way vehicle that day was—unfortunately for him—a bicycle."

Joe's face darkened. "Goddamn brother-in-law stole my car. Can you believe that?"

Nigel nodded sympathetically. "As the Bard said, it's a shame when there is no honor among thieves."

Joe eyed Nigel suspiciously. "I don't know who this Bard is, but it sure sounds like he knows my brother-in-law."

A tight, nasal-sounding voice came from the other room. "Joseph? Who is at the door?"

"It's Nic and Nigel, Aunt Olive," Nigel called out. "And we have a little surprise for you. We've got an addition to the family now!"

Joe took our coats and then left, muttering something about "seeing if there were any carrots for our horse." Nigel led Skippy down a hallway into a large, expensively furnished room. It boasted a lofty, panoramic view of New York's skyline, which allowed Olive to survey the city without actually having to hear it or smell it. In deference to the season, a perfectly shaped Christmas tree stood to the right of the windows, its branches covered with delicate silver ornaments from Tiffany's. Several festive and professionally wrapped presents were artfully strewn on the floor underneath.

I rounded the corner just in time to see Olive's pinched face bunched in an expression of horror. Olive's feelings about me were no secret. Mostly she regarded me as she would a sour cherry in her nightly Manhattan. She still harbored hope that Nigel would come to his senses and leave me for a woman of "class." A baby would definitely throw a wrench into that hope. While Nigel and I had no immediate plans to start a family, seeing Olive's reaction made me suddenly long for the day when we would. Until then, Skippy would have to do.

"Hello, Aunt Olive!" said Nigel. "This is Skippy. Isn't he magnificent?"

Olive was perched in her favorite spot, an oversized wingback chair. The gold and cream toile upholstery depicted various scenes of impoverished peasants either killing fowl or aimlessly wandering about the French countryside. When set against this backdrop, I thought that Olive's petite frame, perfectly coiffed blonde hair, and immobile forehead all conveyed a sense of displeased royalty. Nigel disagreed. He thought it suggested irregularity.

At the sight of Skippy eagerly advancing on her, Olive jumped up and darted behind the chair. Skippy climbed onto the now-vacant seat, leaned his head over the back, and proceeded to lick Olive's face with unprecedented enthusiasm. Olive responded with a muted whimper. Skippy: 1; Olive: 0.

"I believe he likes you, Aunt Olive," said Nigel. Skippy barked in apparent agreement.

"Wherever did you find him?" Olive asked, her voice small.

"At the rescue shelter," answered Nigel. "Can you believe it? Just because he has no control over his bladder and a *teensy* case of rabies, his owners were going to put him down. Granted, there was that rather unfortunate incident at the Children's Aquarium, but if you ask me, the seahorses are overrated anyway."

Olive squared her narrow shoulders and fixed Nigel with a tolerant smile. "I have known you far too long to believe that anything you say is serious, Nigel. Now please get that dog off my chair."

Nigel obliged, pulling Skippy down from the chair. "Skippy, go read your book, and let us adults talk a bit." Skippy obligingly redistributed himself on the couch. "Good boy," Nigel said.

Olive gave up on Nigel and turned her attention to me. "Hello, Nicole," she said. "How nice to see you again." Olive called everyone by his or her given name, regardless of personal preference. She considers monikers to be common and therefore refuses to use them. The only exception to this rule was her husband; she called him "Max." For Olive, this was tantamount to a daily proclamation of love.

Olive regarded me with a critical eye. "You've let your hair grow, I see. It looks much better shoulder-length. The other cut was too masculine. Besides, red hair never looks good when worn short."

"Yes, I believe you mentioned that. How are you? You look well," I lied, thinking that she was far too thin.

"I am *not* well, thank you. Who could be well during this atrocious time? I gather Daphne brought you up-to-date about this terrible business with Audrey?"

"Yes, she mentioned something about it. I take it Audrey's husband Leo is MIA?"

Olive's thin nose wrinkled, either in distaste at the mention of Leo or my use of what she referred to as "vulgar police jargon."

"Yes," she said. "He's nowhere to be found, and Audrey is desperate. She says she won't go to her party—which has been planned for months—unless he is with her."

"Seems rather dramatic," I said.

Olive paused, appearing to fight her natural instinct to reprimand me for speaking ill of the family. With some effort, she slowly nodded her head in agreement. "Yes. I would tend to agree with you on that. She is very emotional right now and not thinking clearly."

I raised my eyebrow at Nigel. Olive never agreed with my opinion in matters of the Martini family. Nigel raised his eyebrow right back. "Are you feeling all right, Aunt Olive?" he asked. "Why don't you sit down? Skippy won't bother you anymore." Glancing at Skippy's recumbent form, he added, "*Probably.*"

With a wary glance at Skippy, Olive slid back into her chair. "Where's Max?" Nigel asked.

"In his study. He had to take a phone call. Again. There's some sort of crisis at work. I don't know what, but he's been on the phone practically all day with those people at Meyers. They are a nightmare of a client, but we can't afford to lose them." Olive rubbed her hand across her forehead. "I need a drink," she added, before calling, "Joseph!"

Joe appeared immediately, leading me to suspect that, afraid I'd reveal his shady past, he'd been listening from the hallway. "Yes, Ma'am?" he asked with unnatural meekness.

"Please bring out the drinks cart," said Olive. "And let Mr. Beasley know that our guests are here."

Joe responded in a maneuver that appeared to be half bow, half neck spasm before disappearing into the kitchen. "When did you hire Joe?" Nigel asked with the bland intonation of one merely making polite conversation.

"Joseph," Olive corrected. "A few months back. Janet Harris referred him to me."

Nigel's brows pulled together as he tried to place the name. "Is this the Janet Harris that you had that blow out with over the chairmanship of the Hurricane Relief charity ball?"

Olive bristled. "I wouldn't call it a blow out," she said. "It was a minor disagreement."

"I don't know if calling someone an addled, monkey-faced nitwit can be categorized as a disagreement. Especially when those remarks are read into the committee minutes."

Olive shrugged. "That's all forgotten now."

"I'm sure it is," Nigel agreed with a faint smile.

Olive placed a slender finger against her right temple and gently rubbed. "Oh, why couldn't Audrey have married Tobias?" she asked. "Everything would have turned out so much differently."

Tobias "Toby" Addler was a friend of Audrey's from college. He was a bright, ambitious, and generally affable young man. He was also short, balding, and had the beginnings of a potbelly. Olive had long harbored a hope that the two would marry, but then Leo came along and her plans were ruined. It was unclear if she was more upset at the failure of her carefully laid plans or that Audrey had married a bounder. Audrey's hypocrisy at marrying a boy toy while crying that he married her for her wealth seemed lost on Olive.

Olive let out a heavy sigh. Turning to me, she said, "I understand that Daphne spoke with you this afternoon. I only have one question. What do you plan to do to find Leopold?"

FIVE

It took me a second to realize that she was referring to Leo. I shoved Skippy over a few inches, which was no easy task, and sat down next to him on the couch. "I don't know. How long has he been gone?"

"Three days," answered Olive.

"Have you called the police?"

"No," Olive answered with a frown. "This is not a matter for the police. Leopold is off somewhere with some trollop. He's done it before, and I'm sure he'll keep on doing it. However, his sense of timing is appalling, which is why we've asked you here for dinner tonight."

"Actually," said a male voice from the doorway, "we asked you here because we've missed you."

I looked over to see Max, a drink in his hand and a sympathetic smile on his lips. Having come to this family from humble beginnings like myself, Max was a kindred spirit. Tall and solidly built, he had short brown hair that was steadily receding, a ruddy complexion, and wire-rimmed glasses that housed nearsighted, pale blue eyes. He was wearing a rumpled blue pinstripe suit, leading me to believe that he'd only recently returned home from his office. The lines around his eyes had deepened since I'd last seen him. I couldn't tell if it was due to age or exhaustion.

"Hello, Max," I said, standing up. "How are you?"

"Better now," Max said as he gave me a hug. "You are a sight for sore eyes, my dear. But then, you always are." He turned to Nigel and shook his hand. "Good to see you, too, Nigel." Then he noticed Skippy. "Forgive me," he said conversationally, "but what the hell is that on the couch?"

"That's Skippy," I said. "Nigel got him today. Apparently, the man at the pet shop said I wouldn't like the piranhas."

Max nodded, still staring at Skippy. "I can believe that."

"Besides, they wouldn't stay on the leash," Nigel said. "Actually, they *ate* the leash."

"Well, God gives us signs, you know," Max agreed affably.

"Oh, for God's sake, Max," snapped Olive. "We are not here to discuss their dog. We are here to discuss what we are going to do about Leopold!"

Max turned to her. "I've already told you what I think we should do about Leo. And that's nothing. Let's hope he stays away for good this time. However, one option might be to feed him to those piranhas Nigel found. That would seem to be a win/win solution to me."

"Be serious, Max," Olive implored. "You know that Audrey won't go to the party unless Leopold is with her. And to go ahead with the gala without the guest of honor would be unthinkable. It would be a disaster! Do you realize how many people—*important people*—

are coming? We simply can't cancel at this late date. It would be lunacy."

"No," countered Max, after draining his glass. "Lunacy is throwing a huge birthday party the week of Christmas. Lunacy is trying to bring Leo back into Audrey's life." He looked down at his now-empty glass. "Lunacy is having this conversation without a drink. Where's Joe?"

"*Joseph* is getting the drinks cart now," replied Olive.

Max raised his eyes to mine. "I see. And what did *you* make of our new hire, Nic?" he asked, a glimmer of suppressed laughter in his blue eyes.

I was saved from an answer by the sound of the front door opening and then, just as quickly, slamming shut. Moments later Daphne strode confidently into the room. She yanked her fur-trimmed hat off her head and threw it onto an empty chair before giving her father a peck on his cheek. "Hello, everyone," she said briskly to the rest of us.

Trailing in her wake was another woman, this one much less assured. It was Audrey. Pale and delicately boned with fine, almost white blonde hair cut into a pixie, she stared uncertainly at us with mournful brown eyes that appeared red and swollen from recent crying. Unlike her cousin, she stood silently, almost uncertainly at the room's edge. Catching sight of Skippy, she produced a timid smile and moved toward him, her hand extended. Skippy thumped his tail and presented his mammoth head to be petted.

In a family that was equal parts confidence, charisma, and bull-headedness, Audrey was the odd duck. She had inherited none of her mother's breezy charm or her father's steely determination. She was shy and easily swayed. Her only real passion, before Leo that is, was animals. She might struggle to interact with people, but put her in a room with a cat or dog and she suddenly lights up. Most of her time and effort went into her charity organization that worked to find homes for abused and abandoned animals. It was there that traces of her father's famed hardnosed business attitude could be detected. But then along came Leo and all that changed. Not only did she spend less time working for the charity but she had to get rid of her own cats as Leo was allergic.

Behind her was a third addition to the group: Toby Addler. Although only a year older than Audrey, he seemed at least ten. Granted, he was a little balder and heavier than when I'd last seen him—traits that rarely suggested youthfulness—but it was more than that. Toby was what my mother would call "an old soul."

Toby quickly said his hellos, politely shaking both Nigel's and my hand, before stepping back behind Audrey. There, from a respectful distance, he watched her with mournful eyes.

"Hello, Audrey," I said, as I moved to her. "How are you?"

Audrey squeaked out a faint "fine" just as Nigel enveloped her in an awkward, one-sided hug. "Hey, kiddo. It's good to see you again," he said. Audrey murmured something incoherent into his shirt collar.

Shrugging out of her fur-trimmed wool coat and tossing it over her hat, Daphne looked at her mother and then at me. "Well?" she demanded. "Are you going to do it?"

I turned to Nigel. "You know, if I had a nickel for every time I've been asked that today..." I began.

"You'd have three nickels," Nigel said.

"Doesn't seem so impressive when you put it that way," I conceded.

"It's this new math. It's worthless. However, I think the more important question is one that Audrey needs to answer," said Nigel, looking down her. "Do you really want Leo found? You may discover that life is better without him."

Audrey's eyes immediately welled with tears. "No. It won't be. Don't you understand? I love him. I know he has his faults, but then so do I." Her small voice rose to a chipmunk-like pitch, causing Skippy to cock his head at her in confusion. "I *will* make this marriage work. I have to." She lowered her head and in a soft whisper added, "He's all I have. He's my life."

Toby, still standing out of Audrey's sight, reacted as if he'd been slapped.

I sat back down on the couch. Leo was an opportunistic louse, and Audrey was a naïve heiress. Earlier I had considered helping Audrey, but now I saw no reason why I should reunite her with someone who would ultimately drain both her savings account and the remaining tatters of her pride. I knew that Olive regarded members of my former profession to be rough, hardened maladroits whose dealings with the uncivilized factions of society rendered them unfit to mingle with the remaining civilized segments. Or to use my vernacular: dirt bags. Most times, I liked to let her think I was such a heartless misfit. I may have even encouraged it from time to time. This was not one of those times. Returning Leo to Audrey would be like returning a cobra to a mouse. Audrey's blind devotion to Leo was annoying, but I wasn't without some sympathy. I opened my mouth to tell her a polite version of this, but instead I heard, "But of course we'll help you find him. Don't worry. We'll take care of it."

I gaped in mute horror at Nigel, who was now smiling confidently at Audrey. Audrey gave a great sniff and produced a smile; a teary, weepy smile. Nigel threw his arm protectively around her shoulders and winked at me. "Won't we, dear?"

I didn't answer. At best, it seemed a rhetorical question. At worst, it seemed something best left unsaid.

"Good. At least that's settled," said Daphne, fluffing out her flaxen hair. "Now, what's for dinner?"

SIX

Fish still attached to its head was for dinner. I don't particularly enjoy eating food that appears to be watching me as I eat it, but then I usually don't enjoy eating with Olive, either. I chalked it up to a two birds with one stone kind of situation and hoped the Universe took note that I was owed something truly awesome.

"Do you really think you can find him?" Audrey asked as she pushed her uneaten fish around on her plate.

"I don't know," I answered as I did the same with mine. "Tell me about when you last saw him."

Audrey put down her fork. "It was Saturday morning. We had breakfast, and then he said he was going out for a while. He didn't say where. He said he'd be back later that afternoon. We were going to a friend's house for dinner. He never came home."

"Did you have a fight?" I asked.

"No, in fact, Leo was in a particularly good mood. He'd been in one for the last few weeks actually. He was being very ... um, sweet, if you know what I mean."

I did. From the way everyone at the table suddenly put down their forks, I gathered I wasn't alone.

"So, he left without saying where he was going, what he was going to do there, or when he'd be back," I repeated. "And you've no idea about why he was in such a good mood?"

Again, Audrey had no helpful answer. "He just seemed happy. We were getting along. He was looking forward to my birthday party. He'd even begun talking about starting a family."

I glanced at Nigel. From the way his upper lip twitched, I gathered he was thinking the same thing that I was. Leo's recent good mood probably had more to do with Audrey's impending inheritance upon turning twenty-five than a sudden newfound love for his wife. I had no idea what kind of prenuptial contract they had—or even if they had one. As Audrey's trustee, Max would be the one to ask about that. But having a child with Audrey would definitely be a giant plus in Leo's ledger.

"Where do *you* think he is?" I asked.

Audrey stared at her plate. "I ... I don't know really. In the past, there have been times when Leo hasn't come home, but I never asked him where he'd been. I don't know if he'd tell me anyway. But this time it's different. I just know it. While our marriage isn't perfect, he's never taken off for three days in a row. And despite what you think, he wouldn't abandon me on my birthday. I *know* something's happened to him."

I nodded noncommittally. "Do you know any of his friends? Is there anyone you could call?"

Audrey shook her head. "There are some guys that he plays poker with on a regular basis. I've never met them. There is one man I heard Leo talk to a couple of times on the phone. Frank Little. I found

26

his number and called him, but he said that he hadn't seen Leo in over a week." Audrey fell silent and resumed pushing her fish around.

The name rang a bell. If Frank Little was who I thought he was, then Leo could be in serious trouble. "And?" I prompted.

Audrey looked up at me. "And what?"

"What else did Frank tell you? You're holding something back."

Audrey's face flushed. "It's nothing really. He just said something about Leo owing some people money."

"How much?"

Audrey lowered her eyes to her plate, preferring eye contact with a dead fish over me. "Fifty thousand," she said. "Maybe more."

"Dollars?" Olive gasped.

Audrey ducked her head lower. Toby, who was sitting next to her, reached over and put a consoling hand on hers. "Well, I *hope* it's dollars," said Nigel after a moment. "God forbid it's Euros or, even worse, the Pound Sterling. The exchange rate now is terrible for us."

"Nigel, this is serious!" said Olive.

"I think he knows that, dear," said Max. "I think we all know that. Berating the girl isn't going to help any."

"Do you think Leo's disappearance has something to do with the money?" I asked.

Audrey shook her head. "No. He knows I'd pay it. I always pay it. That's why I didn't mention it. It can't have anything to do with his disappearance. He knows he can always come to me."

As Olive began to berate Audrey on the particulars of her marriage, I sat back in my chair and stared at my fish. While Leo might know that he could always get the money from Audrey, the people he owed might not have that same confidence.

SEVEN

After the fish remains were taken off for a decent burial, we retuned to the living room for coffee. Audrey barely touched hers and soon begged off with the excuse of a headache. I didn't blame her. I was starting to get one too.

"Thank you for agreeing to help me, Nic," Audrey said as she put on her coat. Daphne had offered to see Audrey home, but Toby insisted on doing it. He now stood next to her, his sensible black wool coat already on, and ready to go.

"I can't promise anything," I said. "But I will see what I can do. Can you get me Frank Little's number? I'd like to talk to him. Sometimes people are more forthcoming when they're not talking to wives."

Audrey nodded. "Sure, I understand. But I still think you're wrong. I think Frank told me everything he knew. He seemed to want to find Leo too."

Audrey and Toby then said their good-byes with promises to call and left.

After listening for the sound of the front door closing, Olive let out a long sigh. "I hardly recognize her anymore! She's nothing but a walking shell of her former self! Do you know that she's given up all her charity work? She says she just wants to concentrate on Leo! It's ridiculous!"

"Well, there are some who might consider Leo a form of charity work," said Daphne.

Olive ignored her. "Oh, why couldn't Audrey have married Tobias? He's so wonderful to her," she wailed.

"Well, for one, I don't believe Toby ever asked her," said Max.

Olive dismissed this fact with a wave of her hand. "He would have, I'm sure of it. But then Leo came along and ruined everything. Lord, I hate that man. How could Audrey have ever thought Leo was a better man than Tobias?"

Daphne twisted her mouth. "I don't know about that, Mother. If you ask me, Toby is no different from Leo. Just a little more mannered and better dressed."

"Nonsense!" said Olive. "Tobias comes from a good family. And he's devoted to Audrey. Always has been, too."

"You forget, Mother," Daphne countered, "that I've worked with him for the past two years. I know him better than you do."

Olive scoffed. "And since when are you such a expert judge of people? You were convinced that last boyfriend of yours was Mr. Wonderful until you caught him running around on you with that other woman. I told you he was no good."

Daphne flushed a deep red. "You're unbelievable," she bit out through clenched teeth.

"Does Audrey have a pre-nup with Leo?" I asked, before the fight escalated.

Max shot me a grateful look. "Yes. I couldn't stop her from marrying him, but at least I made sure that he agreed to a pre-nup. If they divorce, Leo gets shown the door, and that's pretty much it. He doesn't see a dime."

"Of course, that doesn't help us much *now*. He makes out like a bandit as long as he's still married to her," Olive said. "And it'll only get worse once she turns twenty-five."

"How so?" I asked.

"According to the terms of Audrey's trust, she has limited control over her fortune. For her to spend over the predetermined amount she must first get approval from the trustees," said Max.

"Which is you and Olive," I said.

"Correct," said Max. "However, that all ends once she turns twenty-five. After that, she can do whatever she wants without our approval."

"What is the amount she can spend now without your approval?"

He told me. I let out a whistle. Olive wrinkled her nose in disdain at the noise. "That's still a lot," I said.

"Yes. Yes, it is," Max agreed.

I thought for a moment. "Do you think the reason Leo didn't ask Audrey for the money this time was because he knew it was more than she could pay?"

Max blanched. "God. I hope not."

"What about this Frank Little person?" Daphne asked. "Could we get in touch with him? Do you think he might know where Leo is?"

"He might," I said. "Especially if he's related to Danny Little. Danny is a notorious loan shark. Or at least he used to be when I knew him. He's a ruthless bastard. If Leo ended up on the wrong side of Danny's temper, it could explain his sudden disappearance."

"You mean this man might have killed Leopold?" Olive gasped. "But why? You heard Audrey. She said she always paid his debts. There'd be no reason to kill him!"

I shrugged. "I know. But Danny Little isn't known for his rational thinking when it comes to overdue debts. Or for anything, really. And if Leo couldn't pay his debt this time, Danny might have taken matters into his own hands."

Olive shuddered. "That's horrible. Disgusting. I can't believe the people you associate with," she said.

"*Used* to associate with," I corrected with a smile. "Now, I associate with *you*."

Olive narrowed her eyes, belatedly remembered that I was doing her a favor, and forced a smile on her face.

It was around that time that we all agreed it was time for us to go.

Good-byes were said, airy kisses exchanged, and promises were made to call with news. Then Nigel and I were back in the foyer with Joe. As he helped me into my coat, I grabbed his hand. Hard. "If you want me to keep my mouth shut about what you used to do, Joe, you're going to do me a favor," I said. "Maybe several favors."

Nigel and Skippy waited patiently while Joe mulled this over. Glancing down the empty hallway, Joe said, "What do you want?"

"Well, as I'm sure you know, we were talking about Frank Little tonight. Is he the same Frank Little that's related to Danny Little?"

Joe's eyes widened, but at least he didn't bother to deny eavesdropping. "I told you, I'm straight now. I don't deal with them anymore."

"Yes, I'm sure you're a parole officer's dream, but that's not what I asked. Is he the same Frank Little who is related to Danny?"

Joe paused. "Yeah. Frank's Danny's kid brother."

"See? That wasn't so difficult now, was it? Is Frank still involved in the family business?"

"Yeah. Well, he *was*. A year or so ago, Danny got busted for assault or something. I heard he got three years. Since then, Frank's been working for Fat Saul."

Hearing this left me with an uneasy feeling as to Leo's fate. Fat Saul made Danny Little look like a choirboy. "Thanks, Joe. I'll be in touch," I said.

Joe was pale as he ushered us out. He shut the door behind us with a resounding thud.

I turned toward Nigel and smiled. "Can I just tell you again how much I love your family?"

Nigel winked. "Don't be sarcastic, Mrs. Martini. Aunt Olive says that it does horrible things to your complexion."

"Well, she would know, wouldn't she?"

EIGHT

THE NEXT DAY, NIGEL and I took in a matinee of the latest Broadway hit. It told the story—in three-part harmony—of a man who is tricked into marrying a woman he doesn't love. He refuses to sleep with her so she seduces him in the dark and then leaves. When her disappearance is noticed, the man is accused of murdering her. The woman—and their child—return in time to save him from the electric chair. The man realizes he does love his wife and is happy.

Nigel said it was the stupidest thing he'd ever seen. I said it was based on Shakespeare's *All's Well That Ends Well*. Nigel said that if it weren't for the fact that he was dead, Shakespeare should sue.

Afterward, we joined my friend Marcy Garcia and her husband Arnie for dinner. I had worked with Marcy when I was a detective. Marcy was still working homicide. Arnie taught at a private school for wealthy children who'd been expelled from every other school they'd attended. Each maintained that the other's job was easier.

"So, how did you two meet again?" Arnie asked, as Nigel sampled the sommelier's suggestion.

"Rehab," Nigel answered after taking a sip and nodding his approval.

I laughed as I saw Arnie's eyes grow wide. "Physical rehab," I clarified. "I was recovering from a gunshot wound, and Nigel was recovering from a skiing accident."

"Tree jumped right out in front of me," Nigel explained.

"Which is one of the many reasons we live in L.A.," I said. "There are fewer leaping trees."

"And they only attack celebrities," said Nigel.

Arnie laughed. "I think as a Martini, you qualify as a celebrity. From what I hear, your family could buy and sell New York."

"Well, thankfully they didn't. I shudder to think how my aunt would redecorate it if she had."

"Toile," I suggested.

Nigel nodded. "And chrome. Anyway, in L.A. there is so much obscene wealth, the Martini family's pales in comparison."

"So, you work in movies?" asked Arnie.

"I work with *old* movies; specifically, film restoration. A lot of old movies were destroyed by fire or, worse, just left to rot out of indifference. My company works to find them and salvage what we can."

"How did you get into that?" asked Arnie.

"My mom is a huge movie buff. Growing up, I watched just about every movie ever made. During college, I interned at The Film Institute and later started my own company."

"Nigel's company has restored over two hundred movies so far," I added. "Which was a perk for me on those days when my leg ached too much to move. Nigel would bring over a movie and a bottle of wine and we'd watch these great old films."

The waiter arrived, and Nigel and Arnie turned their attention to placing our orders. As they did, Marcy turned to me and said, "You look great, Nic. But then you always do. You were the most glamorous detective in the department." She looked admiringly at Nigel's profile. "I never thought you'd leave New York, but now I see why you did," she said in a low voice. "But I still can't picture you as a West Coaster. Are you sure you don't miss the Department? You were one of the best."

I shook my head. "Not a chance. I'm done with all that. I never thought I'd like the West Coast either, especially L.A., but I really do. Besides, I have my plate full just trying to block all the starlets who throw themselves at Nigel. He seems to attract them like flies."

"Attracting flies doesn't sound like a compliment," said Nigel. "Besides, you exaggerate. One silly girl threw herself at me. And, if I remember correctly, she had buckteeth and a lazy eye. You had nothing to worry about."

"So, had she been attractive, I might have had something to worry about?" I teased.

"That depends—how attractive are we talking about?"

I stuck my tongue out at him. "Well, until the right one shows up and you kick me to the curb, I'm done being a detective."

Nigel leaned over and kissed me on the cheek. "I'd never kick you to the curb, dear. You know that. As a gentleman, I'd have you escorted. And besides, you aren't done being a detective. You just took on a new case, remember?" Turning to Marcy he said, "Nic's agreed to find my cousin's missing husband. Though for the life of me, I can't imagine why she'd want him found."

"I'm sure I'll find him holed up with some bimbo or hiding out from Frank Little. Or both."

"Audrey has excellent taste in men," said Nigel. "That is if your taste runs to gold digger losers."

"Wait. Frank Little?" asked Marcy. "The one related to Danny Little?"

"Yeah, he's Danny's little brother," I said. "Why?"

"Because Danny Little was paroled this morning. Got out early for—get this—good behavior."

"Good behavior? That sociopath?" I said. "You've got to be kidding!"

Marcy shook her head in sympathy. "I know. You don't have to tell me. But the prisons are overcrowded, and Danny Little can afford the best legal representation."

"Who was his lawyer?" I asked.

"Flynn Sawyer."

Flynn Sawyer was a high-profile attorney. Known for his garish suits, bombastic TV ads, and sleazy tactics, he was a defendant's dream and a prosecutor's nightmare. The city was plastered with his billboards and ads that featured his grinning face and promised a "Win With Flynn."

"That cheap suit?" I said. "I can't believe that man is still allowed to practice law."

"I know," agreed Marcy. "The sad part is that he's raking it in hand over fist. He just bought himself a luxury yacht. Named it *Soft Tissue Damage*."

"Very nice." I said. "I heard that Frank is working for Fat Saul these days. Is that true?"

Marcy nodded. "That's what I heard. When Danny went to prison, Frank made a deal with Fat Saul."

"Any idea what Danny thought about that?" I asked.

Marcy shrugged. "Your guess is as good as mine. Under the terms of his parole, he's not allowed to be near any gambling facilities, which, of course, is the bread and butter of his business. He convinced the parole board that he's going to be managing the family restaurant now."

"That's still in business?"

Marcy took a sip of her wine before answering. "Apparently. Though I suspect it's a front. I mean, would you willingly eat at a place called *Little's Vittles*?"

Next to me, Nigel laughed. "I would. Absolutely. In fact, I think I might have to insist on it."

"Well, we might have to if Leo doesn't turn up soon," I said.

Marcy laughed. "Well, in that case, avoid the veal. I hear it's anything but veal."

"Duly noted," I said.

NINE

THE SCENE THAT MET us when we returned to our hotel room was utter bedlam. Chairs were upended, cushions were ripped, and covering it all was a fine layer of potting soil. The origin for the latter—a large ficus tree—lay across our bed, its branches limp and torn.

Our first thought—that we'd been robbed—was quickly discounted once we saw Skippy. Poised on the loveseat opposite the bed, his fur smeared with potting soil, Skippy warily eyed the ficus tree as if he feared it might attack. Seeing us, he leapt up and barked excitedly, his tail thumping against the couch cushions.

"Um … good boy?" Nigel ventured.

I folded my arms across my chest. "I know we're supposed to be a united front with him," I said. "But I don't see this as a good boy moment."

Skippy jumped off the couch and pranced happily over to us. Nigel patted his head. "He was just trying to protect us," he said.

"From a ficus tree?"

"I'm sure he meant well."

"I'd hate to see what he'd do if he didn't like us so much."

I stared down at Skippy. His tail thumping happily, his tongue hanging out to one side, his eyes returned my gaze with an undeniably proud gleam. I sighed and scratched him behind his ears. Skippy: 45; Me: 0. "Fine, but you are explaining this mess to the front desk," I told Nigel.

An hour later, Nigel, Skippy, and I were settled in our new room. One without a ficus tree. Or any kind of shrubbery for that matter. I didn't know how Nigel explained everything to the hotel staff, but based on a few overheard words and the pitying smiles sent my way, I once again suspected that epileptic seizures played a role.

We opted to stay in for the evening and order room service and watch Bing Crosby and Rosemary Clooney in *White Christmas*. "Did you know that he was twenty-six years older than her?" Nigel asked me as he snuck a hand out to steal one of my fries. I smacked it away.

"Yes, I do. You tell me every year when we watch it. Why would anyone want to wash their hair and face in snow?" I asked, listening to the peppy lyrics.

"I don't know. Although you ask me *that* every year."

"Touché," I said, pushing my plate of fries toward him.

Nigel took one and then raised his glass of wine to mine. "Here's to the hobgoblin of little minds, for we are its poster children."

"I'll drink to that," I said, clinking my glass against his.

"I know," he replied with a smile. "You always do."

———

The next morning, Nigel and I went to pay Frank Little a visit. Skippy came as well, the end result of a mutual agreement between Nigel and the entire hotel staff. According to the address Marcy had given me, Frank lived in an old brownstone on the Lower East Side. The neighborhood had seen better days, but then it probably had seen worse, too.

I climbed the worn steps, knocked on the front door, and waited. After a moment, it swung open. Frank Little stood in the doorway. I knew him to be about forty, but he appeared older. Broad through the waist and narrow between the ears, he had a reputation for family loyalty and stupidity, although it could be argued that this was a redundant description. A limp strand of black hair hung down over his pockmarked forehead. He gazed at me from watery, bloodshot eyes and blinked. His right eye was slightly swollen and bruised. Glancing down at Skippy, he blinked again.

"Hi, Frank," I said. "Remember me? Nic Landis; except now it's Nic Martini."

Frank pulled his gaze away from Skippy and focused on me. "Yeah, I heard you were back in town," he said.

"Did you now?" I said. "And yet, none of the old gang has called or written. Oh, well. I guess that's how it goes."

"I heard you moved out to California and got married," said Frank. "So, who's the lucky lady?"

"Ah, you always were a quick one with the wit, Frank. Can we come in for a minute?"

"What do you want?" he asked.

"We want to come in, Frank," I said. "Come on, now. Pay attention."

Frank looked dully at Nigel. "Who's he?"

Nigel produced a cheerful smile and held out his hand, "Nigel Martini."

Frank ignored Nigel's hand. He narrowed his eyes and pushed the errant strand of hair back up with the rest. "Why do you want to talk to me? I didn't do nothing," he asked.

"I need to talk to you about your pal Leo Blackwell," I answered.

Frank's eyes came into focus. The wheels in his head creaked back to life, and he appeared to come to a decision. Taking a step back, he swung the door open wide. "You got ten minutes," he said.

We followed Frank down a dingy hallway toward the kitchen, where we could hear voices. The décor of the kitchen consisted of battered wood cabinets, stained yellow appliances, and faded wallpaper depicting oversized slices of citrus. At a sticky wooden table, sat three men. On the table was a half-empty bottle of whisky and four glasses. From their large frames and dull eyes, I guessed the men to be associates of Frank.

"Jesus," the largest of the three said when he saw Skippy. His head was shaved and resembled a dented bullet. "You buy a horse, Frank?"

"Shut up, Vic. Don't be a moron," Frank said, pronouncing the word as a color rather than an insult. "This ain't a horse. It's one of those fancy English dogs."

Vic took a sip of his whisky. "Oh. Well, why the hell did you buy one of those?"

"Shut up, Vic," said Frank. "This here's Detective Landis," he added, jerking his thumb in my direction. "Except that she don't do that anymore, seeing that she's retired."

The smallest of the men stood up, yanked a rickety chair out from the table, and offered it to me. He had dull blond hair, pencil-thin lips, and a left eye that drooped. "Have a seat, Ex-Detective Landis," he said, his voice almost a drawl.

"Thank you," I said, taking the offered seat. Nigel pulled out his own chair and sat down next to me. Skippy sat down on my other side. He rested his head on the table and stared at the men. "And you are?" I asked the man who had pulled out the chair for me.

"Pete," he said, sitting back down. He didn't offer a last name, and I didn't ask for one. "You don't look like any detective I ever saw," he continued with an admiring glance. "You want a drink?" he asked, indicating the bottle.

"No, thanks."

"Why are you here?" asked the third man. His eyes were hard and his black hair was cut short enough so that the tattoo on his head was visible. It looked like something with talons was perched on his skull.

"I'm looking for Leo Blackwell," I answered. "Do you know him?"

Talons curled his lip in disgust. "Yeah. I know him."

"He's a no-good piece of shit," Vic added.

"Shut up, Vic," said Frank. "She's here to see me, not you." Frank sat down at the last empty seat and poured himself another drink.

"It's been awhile, Frank," I said. "How have you been?"

"Fine."

"I hear that you're working for Fat Saul these days."

Frank stared at me, unsure how to answer. Finally, he said, "Yeah, we do some business together. Why?"

"I just wondered what Danny thought of that arrangement?"

Frank shrugged. "He was fine with it."

42

"How about now that he's out of jail? Is he still fine with it?"

"Who told you he was out?" Frank asked.

"I still have friends in the department. So, what did Danny make of your working for Fat Saul?"

Frank paused before answering. "He's fine with it," he said finally. "Danny's a big boy. Business is business. Even he knows that."

"I think you might be giving him more credit than he deserves," I said.

Frank gave a harsh laugh. "I don't believe in credit anymore," he said, touching his eye.

"Who gave you the black eye?" I asked.

"None of your damn business," Frank grumbled, just as Vic said, "Fat Saul."

"Shut up, Vic," Frank, Pete, and Talons said in unison.

"Well, I won't mention it then," I said. "But it does bring me back to the main reason I'm here. Our mutual friend Leo. Any idea where he might be?"

Frank pulled his lips into a semblance of a smile. "You sure ask a lot of questions. I'd be careful if I were you. Remember, curiosity killed the cat."

"There are some who would argue that's a noble way to go," I said.

"And besides, everyone knows that was a frame-up. Ignorance killed the cat," Nigel said.

Frank stared at Nigel. "And what's your story again?"

Nigel cleared his throat. "Where should I begin? My father was a relentlessly self-improving boulangerie owner from Belgium with low-grade narcolepsy and a penchant for buggery …"

Next to me, Pete laughed. "Hey! I like this guy!" he said.

Frank didn't share Pete's opinion. "Is he for real?" he asked, jerking his thumb toward Nigel.

"We're not sure," I replied. "We're still waiting for the test results. When did you last hear from Leo?'

Frank shifted in his chair. "A few days ago, why?"

"Well, he's disappeared," I said. "Surely, you know that."

Frank nodded warily. "I may have heard something about it."

"I hear he owes you money," I said.

Frank nodded again. "Yeah. He owes me money."

"I told you he was a bad bet, Frank," said Vic. "Leo's nothing but a worm."

"Shut up, Vic," said Talons.

"A lot of money?" I asked.

"Yeah. A lot of money," answered Frank.

I sighed. "Look, Frank. I don't want to be here any more than you want me here. So, why don't you just tell me what happened without me having to prompt you for every single detail, and then you can get back to your business?"

Frank thought this over for a moment. He gave a curt nod. "Fine. Saul got sick of Leo paying off his debt in installments and decided to call in the full loan. Saul told me to take care of it."

"How much did Leo owe?"

The figure Frank named was well north of the amount that Audrey could withdraw without Max and Olive's approval.

"What did Leo say to this?" I asked.

"He took it pretty well, I thought," Frank said. "He promised that he'd get me the money, but said he needed a few days first. Said he had some angle he was working on. He'd never stiffed me before, so I took him at his word. Next thing I know, he's nowhere to be found."

"How did that go over with Fat Saul?"

Frank pressed his lips together. Unconsciously, his fingers reached up to touch his bruised eye. "He was pissed. He blamed me for letting Leo go. He's out for blood. I told him that I could handle it, but Saul wouldn't listen. He says our reputation is on the line and that we have to make an example out of Leo's face."

Next to me Pete nodded. "We're ready to go, too, if you know what I mean. Some jobs you don't mind doing. Bashing in Leo's face is one of them."

Frank glanced at his watch. "Your ten minutes are almost up," he said. "But tell me. Why are you so interested in finding Leo?"

"His wife is worried about him. She wants him home," I said.

"Christ. His *wife*," Frank said. "She's a piece of work. I mean, I know she's loaded and all, but it would take a hell of a lot more than that to make me crawl into bed with her."

"I'll be sure to let her know that," said Nigel. "I imagine it will come as quite a relief."

Frank stopped and glanced at Nigel in some confusion. "Wait. What did you say your name was again?"

"Martini."

"Ain't that Leo's wife's maiden name?" asked Frank.

"Ah, the proverbial penny has dropped, I think," said Nigel with a proud smile. "Yes, indeed it did. Audrey is my cousin. I'll send her your best."

TEN

BEFORE WE LEFT FRANK'S house, Pete patted Skippy on the head and offered me his sincere hope that I found Leo before he and his crew did and "smashed Leo's face in." Vic started to say something, but Talons told him to shut up. Nigel and I said polite good-byes all around and left.

Daphne then called, inviting us to stop over for a visit. She lived only a few blocks from her parents, in a smaller, less toile-inspired version of their apartment. Her décor leaned more toward clean lines and monochromatic colors. She greeted us at the door, but was immediately drowned out by Olive's voice shouting from the other room.

"Is that them?" Olive called. "Ask Nicole if she's learned anything."

Daphne rolled her eyes. "For goodness sake, Mother. Let me take their coats first."

Olive appeared from the other room. "Nigel's coat *is* off," she protested.

"Yes, but Nic's is not," Daphne said.

I handed Daphne the article of clothing in question, and Olive resumed her questioning. "So, what have you found out?"

"You have all the finesse of a bull in a china shop, Mother," Daphne observed as she hung up our coats in the hall closet. Turning back to us, she asked, "Would you like some coffee?"

Nigel and I said we would and followed her into the living room. Along the back wall was a fireplace. On either side of it were two leather sofas; one in black, the other in gray. A rectangular glass and chrome coffee table separated them. Olive took a seat on the black sofa. Nigel and I chose the gray. Daphne excused herself and went into the kitchen. "Well?" Olive prompted as she smoothed out her red wool skirt. "What have you found out about Leopold?"

"He owes a great deal of money to a man called Fat Saul," I replied.

Daphne poked her head out from the kitchen. "Did you say *Fat Saul*? You're kidding, right? There is actually a man named Fat Saul?"

I nodded. "Yes. His name is actually Saul Washington, but that didn't inspire the kind of fear that his business requires. I'm not really sure if Fat Saul does the trick, but it's what he went with."

Olive crinkled her forehead; or at least tried to. "But I thought Audrey said that Leopold owed money to a man named Frank Little. Does he owe money to him as well?"

"No. Frank works for Fat Saul."

"I see. And how much money does Leopold owe this … this Fat person?" Olive asked, her voice sharp.

I told her. She moaned and covered her mouth with her hand. Daphne came out of the kitchen with the coffee tray. She placed it on the table. Looking at her mother askance, she turned to me. "What did I miss?" she asked.

I told her. She, too, looked stricken. "Dear God! That's ... that's obscene!" With shaking hands, she poured coffee into a gray and white cup and handed it to me. She repeated this process for Olive and Nigel. I added cream and sugar to my cup and stirred it. I took a sip and waited for Olive to find her voice.

She stared at her cup for a moment and then stood up and marched into the front hall. "Where are you going?" Daphne called after her.

"To get my purse," she said. "I need a Valium. I feel one of my anxiety attacks coming on." We listened to the sound of her rummaging through her purse. The rummaging stopped, and we heard her mutter, "Goddamnit!"

"Problem?" inquired Daphne, her voice bland.

"I left them in my other purse," Olive replied. She reappeared seconds later and headed for the kitchen.

"Now where are you going?" Daphne asked.

"To find the whisky," Olive replied. "Where the hell do you keep it?"

Daphne stirred her own coffee. "Top shelf over the stove," she answered.

Olive returned and added a healthy splash to her cup. She offered the bottle to the rest of us, but we deferred. Banging the bottle down on the table, she then took a restorative sip of her coffee and closed her eyes. No one spoke. After a moment, Olive opened her eyes again. "I won't do it," she said.

"Do what?" Daphne asked, as if she really didn't want to hear the answer.

"Allow Audrey to pay that money. I simply won't allow it!"

"Imagine my surprise," Daphne murmured as she took a sip of coffee. "But I think you are forgetting something, Mother. After Audrey turns twenty-five, she won't need you or Dad to co-sign anything. The money will be hers outright."

"Nonsense!" snapped Olive. "There must be a way we can stop her!"

Daphne shook her head. "I understand you *think* that, but you *can't*. I know the terms of the trust. It's very simple. Once she turns twenty-five, she controls her money. End of story. There are no loopholes that allow you, Dad, or anyone else to wrest it away from her."

"Do you think that's why Leo went missing?" Nigel asked. "Could he be waiting until Audrey's birthday, knowing that once she has control of her fortune she'll probably pay it off?"

Daphne considered this. "It's a possibility, but I can't imagine if that really were the case that Leo wouldn't have told her his plan beforehand. I mean, to leave her alone and worried hardly seems like a good lead plan before hitting her up for a ton of money."

"That's it," said Olive, rising from the couch. "I'm calling your father."

We sat in silence as Olive marched across the room and rummaged through her purse. Finding her phone, she angrily punched in Max's number. "Hello? Betty? I need to talk to Max. What? Oh. I see. Well, this is Mrs. Beasley. I need to speak to my husband. I see. When do you expect him back? I see. Well, please have him call me when he returns. *Immediately*." She ended the call with a frustrated click and rejoined us in the living room.

"Dad not in?" Daphne asked, her voice mild.

"No. He's not. And what happened to his secretary, Betty?" Olive asked.

"She was let go about a month ago," answered Daphne.

"Why?" Olive demanded.

Daphne's face wrinkled in repugnance. "She was sleeping with a few of our clients. It was disgusting, really. We have our firm's reputation to consider. Can you imagine what it would do to business were it to get out that we employed a slut for a secretary?"

Nigel opened his mouth to answer. I quickly stepped on his foot before he could answer. "That's a rhetorical question," I explained to him.

"Well, why wasn't I told of this?" demanded Olive.

Daphne looked at her mother in confusion. "Why would you be told of this? Had you ever met Betty?"

"Well, no, but if it concerns Max, it concerns me. What did this Betty look like?"

"Blonde, pretty in an obvious kind of way. Wore short skirts, high heels, and if I remember correctly, chewed a lot of gum," Daphne answered.

"And who is his new secretary?" Olive asked.

Daphne laughed. "You just got off the phone with her not two minutes ago, and you've already forgotten her name? Now do you see why no one told you about Betty? The new secretary is named Mary. Mary Crenshaw."

"And what does *she* look like?" Olive asked.

"Gray hair, badly permed," Daphne said. "She wears sensible shoes, support hose, and, I think, dentures."

"Excellent," said Nigel. "No need to worry about any nasty gum-chewing habit."

Daphne grinned. "*Exactly,*" she said.

"I don't see anything funny about this," Olive snapped. "Frankly, I think the three of you are being very unsupportive, sitting here and making jokes."

I raised my eyebrows in surprise. Nigel came to my defense. "That's not fair, Aunt Olive," he said. "Nic has been doing exactly what you've asked—which is to find Leo. It's not her fault that he hasn't turned up yet."

Olive ducked her head a bit. "You're right. I'm sorry, Nicole. I didn't mean to imply you weren't helping."

"You didn't imply it," Nigel corrected. "You said it. And besides, Nic doesn't make jokes. She just laughs at mine."

I smiled at Olive and squeezed Nigel's arm. "Who says chivalry is dead?"

"Shut up, woman," Nigel said. "I wasn't done talking."

Daphne and I laughed. Olive didn't. She seemed out of sorts for the remainder of our visit, which was mercifully cut short after Skippy got into the trash. After fishing several candy wrappers, receipts, and a partially completed ledger out of his mouth, Nigel and I made our excuses and left.

On the way back to the hotel, I bought Skippy a large rawhide toy as reward. He really was becoming one of the family.

ELEVEN

THAT NIGHT, NIGEL AND I went to Mario's, a favorite restaurant of mine from my days with the department. It was a small place tucked away on a side street in Little Italy, but it served the best dish of *linguine con le vongole* anywhere in the city. I was surprised to find that the owner, Gino Santini, remembered me. He was a large man, with a ready smile and mop of bushy auburn hair that was beginning to go gray. He came out from behind the hostess stand and greeted me with a giant hug when we entered. "As I live and breathe! Detective Nic Landis!" he said. "How are you?"

"Hi, Gino. I'm fine. But actually, it's Martini, now. I retired and got married. This is my husband, Nigel," I said, indicating Nigel.

Gino extended his large paw of a hand to Nigel and said, "Well, congratulations to you. Nic, here, was one of the best detectives in the city, and the prettiest too. We miss having her around. But I suppose our loss is your gain."

Nigel said something about agreeing to that, but Gino didn't hear him. He had suddenly noticed Skippy. "What in the name of all that is holy *that*?" he asked.

"That is Skippy," I answered. "He's new."

Gino looked down at Skippy. Skippy wagged his tail, sat down, and presented his paw to Gino. Gino laughed and accepted it. Looking back at me, he asked, "Table for three?"

"Yes, please," I answered.

Gino led us to a table in the back. Although we walked past several occupied tables, no one gave Skippy at second glance. There were some parts about New York that I really missed. Gino seated us at a table in the back corner. He handed us our menus and insisted to treating us to a bottle of wine. As we looked over the selections, I heard someone calling my name. I glanced up and saw Marcy and Arnie walking toward us. "Hello," I said, smiling. "How are you guys doing?"

Nigel stood up and greeted them as well. "Are you here for dinner?" he asked. "We've just sat down. Can you join us?"

They demurred for a few minutes, saying that they didn't want to intrude, but soon we had convinced them to join us. After Gino had taken our orders, Marcy turned to me. "So have you made any progress in finding your cousin's husband?" she asked.

"Cousin-*in-law's* husband," I corrected. "There's an important distinction. But no, we haven't found him. Why? Have you heard anything?"

"Well, I don't know if it's related, but guess who turned up dead this morning?"

"Who?"

"Fat Saul."

"How?"

"Shot."

I wasn't surprised. Fat Saul lived a violent life. It wasn't too hard to guess that he'd come to a violent end.

"Where was he found?" I asked.

"At a building site downtown. It's still under construction, but it's another one of those high-end residential complexes. The flooring crew found him in one of the apartments. The coroner thinks he was killed sometime late last night," said Marcy. She took a sip of wine. "We haven't released the details of his death to the public just yet, so keep this to yourself."

"Sure. Did Saul have any ties to anyone on the work crew?" I asked.

She shook her head. "Not that we can find. But it's early days yet. Besides, Saul wasn't exactly the kind of guy you admitted knowing."

"How was he shot?" I asked.

"I'm going to go out on a limb here and guess, 'with a gun,'" Nigel said. Turning to me, he smirked. "See? I should totally be an equal partner in this. I'm a natural."

"Yes, dear. Very impressive. However, what I meant was, did it seem like an execution or the result of a fight?"

Nigel raised his eyebrows in admiration. "Oh! Good question!"

"From the looks of it," said Marcy, "there had been some kind of struggle. He was shot in the stomach. Bled to death."

"Painful way to go," I observed.

"Yeah. I'm all broke up," Marcy replied. "The way I see it, it's one less psycho I have to deal with."

"Any idea as to who might have wanted him dead?"

"Only half of New York. And not just the dodgy part. Fat Saul was an equal opportunity bastard."

I thought for a moment. "Have you talked to Frank and Danny Little? With Danny out of prison, maybe they wanted to take over the business. When I last saw Frank he was sporting a pretty nasty black eye, a gift from Saul over Leo skipping town. Maybe Frank was tired of taking a beating from someone not his older brother."

Marcy nodded. "Yes. I thought about that too. They both check out. They've got a group of people who swear they were with them all night, not that that means anything. That bunch would swear to Jesus Christ at the Second Coming with their fingers crossed behind their backs. Still, Saul made a lot of money with his business. It's a hard motive to discount."

"How lucrative was his business?" Nigel asked.

Marcy shrugged. "Who knows for sure? I doubt he ever filed a legit tax return. But let's just say that had he visited L.A. before his untimely death, he might have had his fair share of starlets throwing themselves at him."

"It's a shame he missed that," said Nigel.

I poked him. "Be serious," I said, before turning back to Marcy. "Any chance you'd mind if I talked to Frank about this? Not in any professional capacity, of course," I added when I saw her hesitate. "I just think that I ought to convey my sympathies over the recent loss of his business partner."

"In person, I assume," Marcy guessed, with a smile.

"I think it's more appropriate."

Nigel nodded in approval. "Very Emily Post." Giving my hand a squeeze, he added, "Aunt Olive would be so proud of you."

TWELVE

THE NEXT DAY FOUND us once again on Frank Little's doorstep. This time, however, my knock was not immediately answered. I had resorted to leaning on the doorbell when Frank finally flung open the door.

"What do you want, Landis? I mean *Mrs. Martini*," he groused when he saw me. "I thought we were done catching up."

"What can I say, Frank? You enchant me. I want to talk to you about Fat Saul, your dearly departed business partner."

Frank's small eyes narrowed further. "What about him?"

"Well, I heard he turned up dead in a building complex downtown."

"Yeah, so?"

"Do you really want to have this conversation out on your front steps?" I asked.

Frank considered this and then opened the door wide to let me in. "Just ten minutes," he said.

"I know the drill," I answered, as I followed him once again down the hall to the kitchen. As before, Frank was not alone. However, this time there was only one other person sitting at the still-sticky kitchen table. With a frown on his face and a bottle of scotch in his hand, sat Danny Little. Danny was older than Frank by about ten years. Everything about him was an exaggerated version of Frank. His frame was bigger, his hair thicker, and his propensity for cruelness suggested in the more pronounced slant of his mouth.

Seeing me, he began to sputter. "Jesus, Frank! What the hell are you thinking bringing a cop in here?"

"Why, Danny!" I said with a smile. "I'm flattered that you remember me after all these years."

"Aw, ease up, Danny," said Frank. "She's ain't a cop no more. She got her leg shot up and got married."

"It was the only way I could get her to say yes," Nigel explained with an apologetic air. "Drastic, but effective."

Danny turned his attention to Nigel. "And who the hell are you?" he barked.

"Nigel Martini," came the reply.

Danny eyed Skippy next. "What's with the dog?"

"He's a Seeing Eye dog," Nigel said.

Danny looked at Nigel. "You blind?"

"No," Nigel answered. "Why?"

While Danny struggled to make sense of Nigel, I sat down at the table, taking care not to touch the sticky surface. Nigel and Frank did the same. Danny gave up on Nigel and poured out a drink for himself and Frank. No one offered us one. I was not offended.

"I want to ask you about Fat Saul," I said.

"What about him?" asked Frank.

"What happened to him?"

"He got himself killed."

"He did that all by himself?" I asked. "Really? I thought maybe he might have had some help with that."

"Did you now?" Frank asked. "Don't see how it's any of your business."

I sighed. "Frank, the faster you answer my questions, the faster I leave. So, again, what happened to Fat Saul?"

Frank took a large sip of his scotch before answering. "Someone killed him," he finally said. "I don't know who, and I don't know how. The police won't tell me anything. All I know is that they left Saul to die like some animal."

I leaned back in my chair. "Frank, you know as well I do that Saul did far worse to other people over the years. Don't pretend like he didn't have his enemies. There are some who might say his mode of death was fitting."

Danny did not agree with my sentiment. His mouth twisted, and his eyes hardened. He leaned across the table and jabbed his forefinger at me. "I'd be real careful if I were you, Landis," he said. "You're not in the department anymore. That protection is long gone." He made a point of looking at my leg. "Not that it served you too well before," he said with a semblance of a smile. "You never know. Next time, it might be more than just your leg that gets shot up."

"Which reminds me, dear," said Nigel, as he crossed his legs and casually studied his fingernails. "We really should send flowers to that man's grave while we're in town. I know he shot at you first, but it's the decent thing to do."

Danny looked at Nigel in surprise before turning back to me. "Did you kill someone?" he asked. "Really? Because, no offense, but you don't look the type."

"None taken," I said politely.

Nigel patted my hand. "It's what first attracted me to her, actually," he confessed.

Danny blinked in confusion.

"If you're done threatening me, Danny, I'd like to ask Frank a few questions," I said. "What do you know about Fat Saul's death?"

"I told you," Frank said. "Nothing. Someone killed him. End of story."

"Not a very good story," I said. "I think it needs more detail. For instance, let's add in a man named Leo Blackwell."

"Who's that?" asked Danny.

"He's the reason your brother has a black eye," I said. "Didn't Frank tell you about him?"

Danny looked questioningly at Frank. "What is she talking about?"

Frank waved his hand as if to brush away the question. "It's nothing. Leo's just some mark. He owed me and Saul some money. Saul wanted me to collect, and I told Leo he had to pay up. Leo said he needed a few days, and I said okay. Leo took off, and Saul got mad."

"Saul give you that black eye?" Danny asked.

"Yeah," Frank said.

"Good thing he's dead then," said Danny. "How much does this Leo guy owe?"

Frank told him. Danny's eyes widened. "Jesus. No wonder Saul was mad. Hell, I'd have clocked you too if you'd let that kind of money get away from me."

"You always were a businessman first, Danny," I said. "Have you heard anything from Leo, Frank?" I asked.

Frank took a sip of his drink. "Nothing. As far as I know he's still hiding."

"And what about the money he owes?"

Frank sat back in his chair. "I'm in charge of the business now, and as far as I'm concerned, Leo owes me that money and a little more, if you know what I mean."

"I think I get the general idea. Any chance Saul might have been out looking for Leo when he was shot?"

"He might have been." Frank's eyes narrowed. "Why, you think *Leo* had something to do with Fat Saul's death? He might hit a woman, but I can't see him killing a man."

"Well, that certainly is a noteworthy defense," I said. "But even so, I'd like to talk to him. Any idea where he might be?"

Frank scoffed. "Seriously? You think if I knew that, we'd be having this conversation? Trust me, if I knew where Leo was, then you would too. He'd be at the hospital."

"Fair enough," I asked. "Do you know what Saul was doing last night?"

Frank shook his head. "He wouldn't tell me. All I know is that he got a call and took off without saying anything."

"Who called him?" I asked.

Frank shook his head. "I don't know. I wasn't with him when he got the call. One of the guys said that they thought it was a woman."

I thought about that. "Could this woman have been a friend of Leo's?" I asked.

"Maybe," said Frank. "Saul put it out there that we were looking for Leo, and that we'd pay to find him. Lots of people happy to make a little extra cash this time of year."

Danny shifted in his chair. "Why are you here harassing my brother?" he asked me. "He hasn't done anything. Don't you have something better to be doing?"

"Well, now that you mention it, there are a few restaurants I've heard a lot about. Maybe I should check those out. Ever hear of Little's Vittles? I wonder if my old friends in the department would like to meet up there."

Danny glowered at me. "There's nothing going on there. It's clean."

"I assume you mean that figuratively."

"I dare you to prove otherwise!" Danny shot back.

I turned back to Frank. "Frank," I said, "You want to find Leo. I want to find Leo. For different reasons, of course. But the only way you are ever going to get your money is if Leo goes home to Audrey. Now, is there anyone who might be able to help me?"

Frank didn't answer right away. He appeared to be debating some matter in his head. It could have been whether to tell me the truth, or whether to scratch a particular itch. Only time would tell. After a moment of internal debate, he looked at me. "Leo liked to have a good time, but he wasn't real particular or steady about who he hung out with, if you know what I mean."

I said that I did. "But?" I prompted.

He paused. "Well. Yeah. There is someone. But I've already talked to her. She doesn't know where Leo is either."

"That may be so, but I'd still like to talk to her."

Frank slowly nodded. "Fine. If it helps me get my money, I'll tell you. Lizzy. Lizzy Marks."

"Lizzy?" said Danny. "Our Lizzy?"

Frank nodded. "Yeah."

Danny started to say something else but stopped himself. "This Lizzy was Leo's girlfriend?" I asked.

Frank shrugged. "Might have been. Might not have been. Lizzy isn't a one-man gal, if you know what I mean."

"I do. How does she know Leo?" I asked.

Frank shrugged again. "I think she met him through some job she had."

"Do you know what job?"

Frank shook his head. "No. I just knew it was some business downtown. A legit one, too," he added proudly. "She's real smart."

Danny frowned. "Lizzy went legit? Seriously? Since when?" Danny's face held an expression of profound disappointment. Not unlike a parent discovering their golden child has taken up shoplifting.

"I didn't say *she* went legit," Frank clarified. "I said she was working at some place downtown that *was* legit. At least on the outside. She got wind of some embezzling scheme her boss was involved in. She's cashing in on it."

Danny smiled, his faith restored. "Lizzy could always sniff out a scam."

"I take it that you know her well?" I asked.

"Yeah," said Frank, taking a sip of his drink. "We grew up in the same neighborhood. She's a looker and always knew how to attract the guys. Problem was that she had lousy taste. Her first husband ended up in jail and so did her second, come to think of it."

"Well, some girls always go for the dangerous guys," I said.

Frank shot me a funny look. "Hell, Landis. In our neighborhood, everyone was dangerous. Lizzy just always seemed to go for the guys that didn't have the brains not to get caught."

"Ah, it's a subtle distinction, but I get it now," I said.

"That guy, Mickey, she went with didn't end up in jail," Danny pointed out.

"Yeah, but he got himself killed," Frank said. "Like I said, lousy taste. It's too bad, too, because Lizzy's got brains. She always knew how to work someone. As a kid, she'd just smile real big and be able to get whatever she wanted. She probably would have made a fortune by now, but she always let herself get screwed by some asshole."

"And now she's with Leo?" I asked.

"Yeah. From what I heard," Frank said. "But when I called to tell her about Fat Saul, I asked her about him, and she said she hadn't heard from Leo in awhile."

"Did she say anything else?"

Frank scratched his head. "Said her ex-husband was bothering her. She was thinking about changing her name or something."

"Who is this ex?" I asked.

"Billy," said Frank. "Billy Morgan."

Danny looked up in surprise. "Lizzy married Billy? That idiot?"

Frank nodded. "Yeah. I know. Anyway, it's over. He was working some insurance scam a few years back. Got sloppy and got five years. Lizzy divorced him while he was in prison."

Danny shook his head in disbelief. "Billy Morgan ..." he left the thought hang unfinished.

Frank nodded. "I know. Billy's worthless. A couple of times I offered to make him disappear, but that's not Lizzy's style. She's good that way, you know?"

"She sounds like a real gem," I agreed.

"She should have taken me up on my offer," Frank said. "Billy got out of prison early for good behavior. As soon as he did, he beat the crap out of her for divorcing him."

Next to me, Danny shook his head. "Some system we have. It's always the rats who get out early."

"Cheers to that," said Frank before draining his whiskey.

Neither of them seemed to appreciate the irony in that statement. I decided not to enlighten them.

THIRTEEN

FRANK GAVE ME LIZZY's address, and Nigel and I said our good-byes. "You certainly know the most interesting people," Nigel said once we were outside. "They are an absolute delight!"

"Oh, please," I said. "I have three words for you—your Aunt Olive."

Nigel tipped his head thoughtfully. "Do you suppose there's any way that we can introduce your Frank Little and his crew to my Aunt Olive?" he asked. "I would happily exchange all my Christmas presents for the chance to watch that."

"Be careful what you wish for, my dear. The way this week is going, I wouldn't be surprised by anything."

According to Frank, Lizzy lived in the West Village. Before we paid her a visit, I called Marcy to tell her about Fat Saul's mysterious female caller. "So, he got a call from someone right before he went out?" Marcy asked. "Do you really think it's connected to his death?"

"I don't know. Probably not. But then again it might be. I just thought I'd pass along the information."

"Okay," she said. "Thanks. I'll see if we can find anything out from the cell phone records. Any luck in finding your cousin's husband?"

"Again. It's my cousin-*in-law's* husband. I stand by that distinction. And no. He's still missing."

"Okay. Well, keep me posted. I'll let you know if I hear anything." I thanked her and hung up. Nigel said that he wanted to eat lunch and do some more Christmas shopping before we visited Lizzy, so we headed over to Fifth Avenue. Along the way, Nigel stopped at a pet store and bought a pair of reindeer antlers for Skippy. By the time we reached Rockefeller Center, Skippy had been patted by three policemen, made friends with two horses, goosed several ladies who turned to glare at Nigel and then ended up smiling, and been introduced to three children as one of Santa's reindeer out doing last-minute reconnaissance work for the Big Man. We pushed our way through the noisy crowd and paused to watch the skaters skim across the ice rink where the hum of tourists' conversations, Salvation Army bells, and Christmas music filled the air.

"I know it's cliché," said Nigel, "but I do love New York at Christmastime. The buildings are lit, the windows are decorated, and the people are *nice*."

"They may be nice, but there are still too many of them," I said, as my side was assaulted by yet another bag loaded with boxes. "I need a cup of something strong and a place to sit," I added as I pulled my coat tight against the cold evening air.

"Your wish is my command," said Nigel. "Skippy, lead the way." We headed up Fifth Avenue, passing a Salvation Army volunteer as we did. Nigel paused and shoved a handful of bills into the bucket.

"Thank you," said the young man as he rang his bell. Nigel nodded, "Merry Christmas," he replied. We were a few feet away when I heard the man cry out in surprise, "Hey!"

Nigel kept walking. I glanced up at him. "Nigel, how much did you put in the bucket?"

"It's Christmas. You're supposed to be generous."

"Nigel. How much?"

He shrugged. "A few hundred."

"A *few*?"

"Okay, six."

"*Six hundred dollars*? Are you crazy? Why on earth are you walking around with that kind of money? And here of all places!"

"You're being a Grinch. It's Christmas. It's not like we can't afford it. Just enjoy the atmosphere."

I sighed. "I know you think I'm a Grinch," I said as we squeezed through the crowd, "but you didn't grow up here. And after awhile, even Rockefeller Center overloads the senses. It's too much of everything. The crowds, the music, the incessant ringing of bells ..." I paused.

Nigel paused as well. We looked at each other. Then we looked down at Skippy. Skippy looked up at us. In his mouth was a large Salvation Army bell.

"Oops," said Nigel.

"Big oops," I agreed.

Nigel began to wrestle the bell out of Skippy's mouth. "Bad dog, Skippy," he said. "No. Give me the bell. Skippy, give me the bell!" Skippy, however, treated Nigel's pleas as part of a grand new game. He artfully dodged and ducked our attempts to retrieve the bell, which clanged merrily all the while. After a few minutes, Nigel put his hands on his hips and stared at Skippy. Skippy stared back, his tail still wagging, and the bell still ringing. Without a word, Nigel turned around and pushed his way back into the crowd. When he emerged again, he calmly took Skippy's leash and resumed our walk.

"What did you do?" I asked.

"I bought us a bell. Merry Christmas."

FOURTEEN

Next we headed to Lizzy's apartment in the West Village. Nigel finally found a cab driver who would take Skippy. Initially, Skippy climbed into the front seat, but the driver quickly advised us not to press our luck, and so Nigel sat up front while Skippy and I squeezed into the backseat. After giving Lizzy's address to the driver, we settled in for the ride. The driver, whose license identified him as Sam, kept a wary eye on Skippy from the rearview mirror. "I imagine you see a lot of strange things in your job," Nigel said politely to Sam.

Sam glanced at Skippy. "Some stranger than others," he said. "Hey, listen. Are you sure he's a dog? 'Cause he don't look like no dog I've ever seen."

"Oh, yes, quite sure," said Nigel. "His mother was my dog growing up."

"Yeah?" replied Sam. "What kind of dog was she?"

"Toy poodle."

Sam sputtered. "Jesus. What kind of dog was its dad?"

"Determined," answered Nigel.

Sam dropped us off in front of Lizzy's apartment. She lived in the West Village, a once-rowdy neighborhood that was trying to shake its frat-boy image. This effort enabled the realtors to charge more for the properties on the basis that it was an "up-and-coming neighborhood." When Nigel asked me what that meant, I told him it meant there were more Starbucks than liquor stores. Nigel sighed, and said he would never understand some people's ideas about progress.

Outside of the building a man stood smoking a cigarette. I had a brief impression of a large frame, hooded eyes, and a beak nose before he saw Skippy. He quickly flicked his cigarette to the ground and walked away. While it was a reaction I was getting used to, I didn't appreciate having to wrest Skippy away from eating the smoky remains.

We entered the lobby of the building and pressed the button for the elevator. As we waited, a middle-aged woman carrying a bag of groceries joined us. Seeing the curious glance she shot at Skippy, who still wore the antlers and proudly held the Salvation Army bell in his mouth, Nigel smiled at her. "He's a ChristmasGram," he said indicating Skippy. "It's a new service the mayor is providing for the city's shut-ins."

The woman continued to stare at Skippy. "Seems to me you're just ensuring that they'll stay shut in," she said.

The elevator arrived and Nigel, Skippy, and I got on. The woman did not. "I'll catch the next one," she said.

Lizzy's apartment was on the tenth floor. As I pressed the button, Nigel asked, "Do you really think we're gong to find Leo here?"

"Doubtful," I answered. "If Leo was hiding from Fat Saul then he certainly wouldn't be stupid enough to hide out at his girl-friend's house. However, she might know something that could help us."

"Fine by me," said Nigel, "But after we're done with Ms. Marks, why don't you come back to the hotel with me. I have some lovely etchings I'd like to show you."

I smiled up at him. "I'd love to. You know how I love your etchings."

Lizzy was home. From the speed with which she answered my knock, I suspected she was expecting someone else. Well, that and the fact that she was wearing nothing but a sheer peach-colored negligee and an expectant smile. I had a brief image of a curvy blonde with lots of tanned skin before the door slammed shut. "Who the hell are you?" she hollered at us.

"We're friends of Leo, Ms. Marks," I answered. "Leo Blackwell? Please, open the door. We need to talk to you."

There was a brief pause. Finally, she answered. "All right. But hang on a second. Let me grab my robe."

Nigel cocked his eyebrow at me. "Is this what you usually en-countered when you had to make house calls?" he asked.

I shook my head. "No. I usually encountered hysterical girl-friends with crying babies."

"Oh," he said, looking back appreciatively at Lizzy's door, "I'm beginning to see what you mean by an up-and-coming neighbor-hood."

A few minutes later, Lizzy opened the door—a little less ex-posed and a lot less enthusiastic. I guessed her to be in her forties—but she wasn't going out without a fight. Her hair was long and wavy, falling well past her shoulders. She had a pretty face, one that appeared to be taut and duly preserved, but it was her body that caught attention. It was somehow both thin and curvy, soft and firm. From the brief glimpse I'd had of her negligee, it was also a body she was proud of. "Okay, now who are you?" she asked as she yanked the belt of her silk robe into a tight bow.

"I'm Nigel and this is Nicole. We're looking for Leo Blackwell," Nigel said. "I'm so sorry to disturb you, but is it okay if we come in for a minute?"

Lizzy's gaze shifted to Nigel, where it remained. Her hazel eyes radiated approval, as well as a few other baser emotions. Nigel produced his most winning smile. Her stance softened further.

"What makes you think I know where he is?" she asked.

"Well, according to our sources…" Nigel brook off. "I do hope we have the right apartment. We have some rather important financial information for Mr. Blackwell that I think he'll be pleased to hear. I'd hate to think we've missed him again."

"No, you have the right apartment," she said, her voice now an octave lower. "I know Leo. Well, come on in. Any friend of Leo's and all that."

She opened the door wide. "Follow me," she said, as she sashayed down a narrow hallway. Nigel and I entered, shutting the door behind us, and followed. The rhythmic sound of her kitten heels on the parquet floor echoed in the small foyer before being swallowed up by the living room's thick wall-to-wall carpeting. There she indicated for us to sit on the red velvet couch, while she took a seat opposite us on a gold damask club chair. Between us was a low, black coffee table in the shape of either a diseased kidney or a wilted lima bean. Apart from the ghastly décor, the apartment was perfectly nice. There was a good-sized kitchen, with new chrome appliances and granite countertops. Off the living room was another room, the door of which was ajar. From my vantage point, I could see a large bed, a bit of a mirrored wall, and a side table. On top of it were two suitcases, partially packed, and several piles of clothes waiting to be added.

Lizzy slowly crossed her long legs, letting her robe slip off them in the process. A tattoo of a dove adorned her left ankle. A kaleidoscope of butterflies decorated the right. I suspected more creatures were soaring in the wings. Lizzy lit a cigarette and slowly exhaled. Her eyes never left Nigel's. "We haven't met before, have we?" she asked after taking a drag. "I think I would have remembered meeting you." Her eyes moved to Skippy. "Especially the dog. He's a bull mastiff, right?"

"That's right," Nigel said. "Well spotted. Not too many people are familiar with the breed."

Lizzy gave a throaty laugh. "Honey, you'd be surprised at the things I'm familiar with. So, how can I help you?" she prompted.

"Well, we're trying to find Leo Blackwell," I said. "I understand you might know him?"

"I know him," she said with a slow smile.

"Excellent! We're on the right track. We can't seem to get hold of him," Nigel answered. "But then we were told to look you up," he paused to cast an appreciative eye over her tanned legs. "They sure didn't exaggerate about you," he added with a wolfish grin.

Lizzy slowly ran her tongue over her full lips and returned the smile. I produced a polite cough. "So, we were wondering if you know where Leo is?" I asked.

Lizzy glanced over at me, almost surprised to find me on her couch. "And who are you?" she asked, her tone a shade less friendly.

"Girlfriend," Nigel answered.

"I also go by Nicole."

Lizzy took another look at me. This one was more searching. Whatever she was looking for she didn't find. "Doesn't look your type," she finally said to Nigel.

"I get that a lot," I answered.

"What can I say?" Nigel admitted with a shrug. "I'm partial to sloe-eyed girls with gimpy legs."

Lizzy looked pointedly at Nigel's ring finger. "Nice wedding ring," she said.

"Thanks," he said, with a wink. "It was a gift from my employer, if you know what I mean."

Lizzy threw her head back and laughed. "Oh honey, do I ever. But let's cut the crap, shall we? You aren't friends of Leo's any more than I'm friends with that pathetic wife of his. You're Nic and Nigel Martini. In town to attend the sainted Audrey's birthday party bash. Don't you two read the papers? You should. You were the lead item today on page six of the *Post.*"

FIFTEEN

NIGEL SAT BACK INTO the couch and crossed his legs. "I told you the *Times* was overrated," he said to me. "You miss all the good stuff."

"Well, now that introductions are out of the way, do you have any idea where Leo is?" I asked.

Lizzy took another drag off her cigarette before answering. "Why the hell should I tell you anything? I don't owe the Martini family one damn thing. They're no better than the rest of us. Bunch of hypocritical snobs."

"From your palpable hostility, I gather that you are acquainted with the family," I said.

Lizzy looked away and shrugged. "Not really, no. Just what I read in the papers. And what I hear. Who told you about me?" she asked.

"Frank Little," I answered. "Seems Leo owed him some money."

Lizzy's eyes widened at this. "And Frank thought that I knew where Leo was? I told him I haven't seen Leo in days. Did he really send you here?"

I nodded. "He said he didn't think you knew anything, but we wanted to double check."

She seemed to relax a little at this. "Well, he's right. I don't know where he is. Frank and I go way back. He knows he can trust me. But why the hell do you care where Leo is? Seems to me that Leo would be the type of guy the Martini family would like to see disappear."

"His wife is worried," I answered.

Lizzy scoffed. "His *wife*. Please. She's not worried about Leo. The only thing that little bitch is worried about is her reputation. She can't stand the idea of him not being there for her silly, little society party. The women in that family are no good. They only like their money. But as much as they have, it's never enough. No amount is."

"The same might be said about Leo," I observed. "However, far be it for me to speculate on the course of true love and all that. I just want to talk to him. Given recent events I thought he might turn up."

Lizzy blew a textbook smoke ring before asking, "What recent events?"

"Fat Saul's death. He was looking for Leo. I don't think it was a social call. With Saul gone, Leo might feel like celebrating. Maybe taking a trip." I looked pointedly toward the suitcases visible beyond the open bedroom door.

Annoyance flashed across her face. "Leo had nothing to do with that," she said quickly.

"Really?" I asked. "And how do you know this?"

"Because I know Leo," she answered. "He may play a bit fast and loose at times, but he's no killer. Leo just likes a good time, is all. He talks big, but he's a softie. I don't know who shot Fat Saul, but it wasn't Leo."

"You knew Fat Saul, too, right?" I asked.

She nodded. "Yeah. I knew him."

"Well, then you know he wasn't the most rational of men," I said. "Especially, where money was concerned."

"Look, Fat Saul is a … *was* a hot head," Lizzy said correcting herself. "He always was. But Leo always paid his debts. That little wife of his was happy to bail him out every time."

"Except that this time she couldn't," I explained. "This time Leo owed more than what Audrey could withdraw on her own. She'd have to get her aunt and uncle to co-sign everything, and Leo knew that."

Lizzy frowned. "How much did he owe?"

When I told her the amount, her eyes narrowed in anger. She started to say something, but stopped. She glanced at her watch. It was an expensive piece, comprised of white gold and diamonds. "Look, I've got to be somewhere," she said abruptly. "I'm sorry I can't help you. I don't know where Leo is. I haven't seen or heard from him in days. And I don't expect to. Like I said. We're friends, but nothing more." She squashed out her cigarette and stood up. "Now, as fun as this has been, I've got an appointment."

"Yes, I can see that," I said after another glance at the bedroom. "Well, thanks for talking to us. If you happen to see Leo, please tell him we're looking for him."

Lizzy was at the door. Opening it, she turned to me and said, "Like I said, I don't expect to see him anytime soon. I'm sure you'll see Leo long before I do."

"I'll be sure to send him your best," I said, before we stepped out into the hall. The door swung shut in our faces with an unceremonious bang. Skippy barked in protest. Turning to me, Nigel said, "Wow. She certainly didn't like *you*."

"I'm all broke up. Interesting what she said, though, don't you think?"

"About my family? Very," Nigel agreed as we made our way toward the elevator. "I wonder if she's met Aunt Olive?"

"I doubt it," I said. "But that's not what I meant. She knew that Fat Saul was shot. But the police haven't released that information to the public yet; not even Frank knew how he died."

Nigel came to a sudden stop and kissed me. "If we weren't already married, Mrs. Martini, I'd ask you again. Now let's go and get a copy of the *Post*. I don't think I've ever been a headliner before."

I kissed him back. "Don't be so modest, darling."

SIXTEEN

As Lizzy had said, we were the lead item on page six. It read:

Nigel Martini is back in town, ladies! However, this time the former playboy of Manhattan has brought along his wife, former detective Nicole Landis. The two were spotted in the trendy bar at the Four Seasons with what some patrons described as a 'small reindeer.' (Bartender! We'd like what they're drinking!) The two are in town for cousin Audrey Blackwell's mega black-tie birthday bash this Saturday. The guest list is rumored to include the former and current mayor, as well as a few Oscar hopefuls. Although Audrey and hubby Leo appear to be happy lovebirds, there are rumors of trouble in paradise. Could Manhattan's latest poor little rich girl be in for more heartache?

Three small pictures ran with the story. In the first, Nigel was coming out of a nightclub. A scantily clad blonde bombshell was draped on his arm. In the second, I was being wheeled out of the hospital after the doctors dug the bullet out of my leg. Gunshot wound to the leg notwithstanding, I looked terrible. I made a mental note never to wear plaid again. The third picture was from Audrey and Leo's wedding. Olive was right. Leo looked like a dirty married bachelor.

"Pretty girl," I said to Nigel when he came out of the shower. I tossed him the paper. He picked it up and glanced at the picture.

"I've always thought so," he agreed. "But you should avoid plaid at all costs."

"I meant the bimbo on your arm, you dingbat."

Nigel looked back at the paper and adjusted his towel. "Her?" He pretended to study the picture. "Oh, yes. I remember her now. Debbie McGuire. We met at the Botanical Gardens' annual Cherry Blossom Festival. Sweet girl. Lovely cherries. Thought 'horticulture' was a charity program."

"I see. And were you able to provide her with any?"

He smiled. "Well, you know what they say. 'You can lead a whore to culture …'"

"Yes, yes," I said, knowing my cue. "But you can't make her think."

He said solemnly, "The Martini family has a long tradition of public works. You know that."

I yanked his towel. "Oh, is that what we're calling it these days?"

———

Later, I called Marcy and told her about my meeting with Frank and Danny Little and also about Lizzy Marks.

"I don't know, Nic. I've been thinking about what Frank told you. He said it was some woman who called Fat Saul, right?" she asked. "He didn't seem to think much of it at the time, but now that Fat Saul is dead, he suddenly tells you about Lizzy Marks."

"You think he's steering us in the wrong direction?" I asked.

"I don't know. I just find it odd that Danny Little is released from jail and then the man who is his biggest competitor and who works with his brother winds up dead."

"I wondered the same thing. But I got the impression that Frank really doesn't know that Fat Saul was shot whereas Lizzy did."

"I admit that is interesting."

"I thought so. Anyway, I wanted to let you know. I'll keep you posted if I find out more."

We said our good-byes and I hung up. Marcy had a point. It made perfect sense for Danny or Frank to kill Fat Saul and take over the business. But in my experience, most murder cases made very little sense.

I sighed and sat back in the chair. I was tired, and my leg hurt. Nigel came over and pulled me out of the chair. "You walked too much today, didn't you?" he said as he gently placed me on the bed.

"Maybe a little," I admitted.

Nigel stretched out my leg. I closed my eyes as he began to expertly massage the muscle. "I know that my family asked you to find Leo," he said, "but if that means you end up aggravating your wound, or anything else for that matter, then I'll put us on the next plane home."

I opened my eyes. His face was serious. I smiled at him. "Don't be silly, darling. It's just a cramp. I'm fine."

"That you are," he said, kissing me lightly on the mouth. "And I'm going to make sure you stay that way."

That evening we met Daphne at the latest trendy club to be favored by the rich and famous. It wasn't that much different from any other New York club. Like those, it sold overpriced drinks and played too-loud music. The bathrooms were nice, with imported marble and gold faucets, but it still didn't merit thirty dollars for a gin and tonic.

Daphne was already there when we arrived and waved us over to her table. "Hi, Nic. Hi, Nigel," she said. "You remember everyone, right?" she went on, gesturing to the crowded table.

I didn't, but didn't really care enough to mention it. From the bar, a sultry brunette in a skimpy tank top and skinny jeans noticed Nigel and jumped off her bar stool. "Nigel!" she squealed before running over to us. She had a round kewpie-doll face and eyelashes that resembled nesting caterpillars. When she got to Nigel, she placed her hands on either side of his face, pulled him close, and placed a wet kiss on his mouth.

Nigel disentangled himself from the woman. "Hi, Casey," he said, wiping the pink lipstick from his lips. "It's … uh … nice to see you again." Turning to me, he said, "Casey, this is my wife, Nic. Nic meet Casey."

"Hi, Casey," I said as I opened my purse. Pulling out a container, I offered it to Nigel. "Here darling, have a Tic Tac."

Casey afforded me a giant, insincere smile. "You'll have to excuse me," she said. "It's just that Nigel and I have quite a history together." She reached up and playfully caressed his cheek.

"That's nice," I said as I reached over and removed her hand. "But sometimes you'll find that history *doesn't* repeat itself. It was lovely to meet you, Casey, but I think you'll find that your friends are anxiously awaiting your return. I would hate for you to disappoint them on our account." I sat down in the chair that Nigel pulled out for me and turned toward Daphne. "So, how are you?" I asked as Nigel echoed my good-byes and took a seat as well. Casey hovered uncertainly for a moment and then returned to her seat at the bar.

Daphne raised her eyebrows in admiration. "Nicely done," she said to me.

"Thank you. As you might imagine, I've had some practice."

Daphne laughed. "I'll bet you have." Addressing Nigel, she adopted an admonishing tone, "You went out with Casey Wendell? *Seriously?* What were you thinking?"

"I can tell you what he was thinking," said a man to Daphne's left. He had a broad face and a slightly crooked nose. He winked at Nigel.

"That's because you're a twelve-year-old at heart, George," said Daphne.

"Yeah, but not anywhere else," he retorted with a hearty laugh.

"That's what you think," scoffed the redhead to his left whom I vaguely recognized as a guest at our wedding.

"You hooking up with twelve-year-olds, Margo?" teased George. "That's nasty."

The waiter came. He took our orders and interrupted George and Margo. I was grateful for both. Once he'd left, Daphne leaned over to me and asked in a low voice, "Any news on Leo?"

"In a way. I haven't found him, but I did talk to some friends of his," I answered.

"Who?"

"I talked to Frank Little again, the guy Leo owed money to, and his brother Danny. Danny is the loan shark I was telling your mother about. He just got out of jail."

Daphne's eyes widened. "Is he the really violent one?"

"That's Danny," I confirmed. "But he's nothing compared to Fat Saul."

"Well, did they say if Fat Saul had found Leo yet?" she asked.

"No. And I don't think he's going to. Fat Saul was killed last night."

Daphne didn't seem to understand my words at first. I couldn't blame her. The music was impossibly loud. "What?" she asked.

I repeated it. "Someone killed Fat Saul last night."

Daphne processed this while the waiter returned with our drinks. I took a sip of mine. Daphne sipped hers as well. "So, if this Fat Saul guy is dead, then why hasn't Leo come home?" she asked.

I shrugged. "Well, Leo still owes the money. Except now he owes it to Frank. But honestly, it's anyone's guess why Leo is still gone. Maybe he didn't leave because he owed money. Maybe there's another reason. You said yourself that he has a tendency to take off when he meets someone he likes."

Daphne frowned. "True. But I don't know. It just seems different this time."

"Why?"

She fluttered her hands. "I don't know. It just does." She took another sip of her drink. So did I. "You said you talked to Leo's 'friends,'" she said. "Who else did you talk to?"

"A woman named Lizzy Marks. Apparently she and Leo are close. Feel free to interpret that any way you want."

Daphne wrinkled her nose in disgust. "No, thanks. I gather she didn't have any news?"

I shook my head. "No. She claimed not to know much of anything, which I don't believe because she grew up with Frank and Danny Little, and she seemed to have a grudge against your family."

Daphne raised her eyebrows in surprise. "Our family? Why? What did she say?"

"Something along the lines of 'the women are all money-grabbing hypocrites and that Audrey is more concerned about her image than Leo's safety.' Does her name ring a bell?" I asked.

"What was is again?"

"Lizzy Marks."

Daphne thought. "I don't think *I* know her. I'll ask Mother. What did she look like?"

I described Lizzy. "In her forties. Pretty. Long blonde hair. Fake tan. She's very fit and not shy about showing off her body. Has tattoos of butterflies on one ankle and a dove on the other."

"That's quite a description," Daphne said. "And you think Leo was having an affair with her? With a woman in her *forties*?"

"She struck me as one of those women that men like. You know the type?"

Daphne exhaled and sat back against her chair. Rolling her eyes, she said, "Oh, yes. I know the type."

SEVENTEEN

Daphne's phone rang and she went to answer it in a quieter spot. I turned to join Nigel's conversation. He was arguing the merits of old movies to a man across the table. "How can you say that, Tom?" Nigel was indignantly demanding to know. "How can you possibly say that the actors in movies before the fifties aren't any good?"

Tom was thin, with olive skin and large brown eyes framed by thick black lashes. He laughed at Nigel. "Dude. Seriously? They're *old*! Half of those movies are in black-and-white."

"That doesn't affect the *acting or the plot*, you moron! Can you honestly tell me that you don't think Humphrey Bogart wasn't a great actor?"

"Who?" Tom asked.

"Humphrey Bogart! He was in *The Maltese Falcon*," Nigel yelled.

Tom shook his head. "I thought we were talking about *movies*, not books." He paused. "No. Wait. *Boggart*? Isn't that from Harry

Potter? I do like *those* movies. But again, my point is made. They were made *after* 1950 and are in *color*."

Nigel stared at Tom aghast. "Good God, man. I don't even know where to begin. Humphrey Bogart was an actor—the likes of which the world will never see again. Google him. You're thinking of a boggart, which, I grant you, is from Harry Potter. But you do know that those were books first, yes? Please tell me yes, for the love of humanity, Tom, please. Tell. Me. Yes."

Tom smiled. "Yes, of course."

Nigel sighed his relief.

"But," Tom went on, "in my experience, the movie is always better than the book, so I rarely read."

Nigel began to sputter, his expression apoplectic. "What? WHAT?"

I gently patted him on the shoulder. "Calm down, Nigel. I know that you have a special love for the classics, but don't forget that you enjoyed the Harry Potter films, too."

Nigel took a large sip of his drink and said, "Yes, but not at the expense of Humphrey-freaking-Bogart."

———

While Nigel and Tom switched topics, now debating which movie earned the title of Best Christmas Movie, a woman named Nan Coswald slid into Daphne's empty chair. Her face was thin and angular, a feature made even more so by the severe pageboy cut of her jet-black hair. Nan was a friend of Daphne's from law school. She was nice enough, but lived and breathed what she referred to as "The Law." It made for some tiring conversations.

"Hello, Nic," she said. "Where's Daphne?"

"She had to make a phone call," I answered. "I'm sure she'll be right back."

Nan nodded. "She's pretty busy these days now that she's with her dad's firm. I think she works longer than anyone else there just so people don't think she's getting preferential treatment."

Next to me Nigel was yelling at Tom. "You cannot possibly put *It's A Wonderful Life* in the same category as *National Lampoon's Christmas Vacation!*"

"That's what *I'm* saying," Tom said. "How can you compete with Cousin Eddie?"

"Do people think she's getting preferential treatment?" I asked Nan.

Nan shrugged. "Some do. People always like to talk. Of course, Max did give her some of his clients to work with. That had to have ruffled a few feathers. Especially when she started working for Meyers and Company." She paused and looked at me meaningfully. I took a sip of my drink.

"Don't tell me you haven't heard of them?" Nan asked.

I took another sip and shook my head.

"*Die Hard* is not a Christmas movie, Tom," Nigel said. "Any more than *Rocky IV* was."

"How can you say that?" Tom countered. "Rocky fought Drago on Christmas Day!"

Nan raised her eyebrows in amazement at my lack of knowledge. "Well, they are one of the biggest clients of the firm," she said. "They mainly deal with commercial real estate, but recently they've branched out into the private sector. Of course, their focus is high-end luxury for the super rich. Some of their homes are just unbelievable. They did one last year that had three swimming pools! But

Daphne is going to run herself into the ground unless she takes her foot off the gas. She's never going to meet anyone working the hours she works."

"She's out tonight," I observed.

"But she's on the phone," Nan countered.

"Maybe it's not work related," I said, not really caring.

Nan laughed. "No, it is. If Daphne were seeing anyone, she'd have told me. Besides, she says she's off men for a while. She got pretty burned by her last one."

"Is that so?" I mumbled while I tried to catch Nigel's eye.

"Yes. He seemed nice enough—but then she found out he was also sleeping with a co-worker."

I finally kicked Nigel under the table. "Ow. What the ...? Oh, hello, Nan! I didn't see you come in," said Nigel. "How have you been?"

"Good," said Nan. "I just settled a case for one of my clients. I would have preferred to have seen it go to trial—I've never lost a court case yet, you know—but the client wanted the money. It was a pretty big settlement."

"Congratulations," Nigel said. "Now, tell me Nan. What would you consider to be the best Christmas movie?"

Nan thought for a moment. "*Miracle on 34th Street*," she said.

Nigel and Tom began debating which adaptation was better just as Daphne returned to the table. "Hello, Nan," she said as she grabbed an empty chair and dragged it to the table. "How are you?"

"Busy," said Nan. "I just settled the Dixon case. How about you?"

"Same," Daphne said. "Hey, did you read the ruling for Cranshaw? Is that going to affect cases that have already been filed?"

Nan answered, some long drawn-out response that didn't interest me. I turned back to Nigel and sipped my drink. As I half listened to Nigel and Tom continue their debate, I looked around the room. Casey Wendell still sat at the bar, occasionally turning in her seat to glance flirtatiously at Nigel. The fifth time she did so, I smiled and waved at her. After that, she stopped.

A few minutes later, I was surprised to see Toby take a seat at the bar. Not so much because he was out, but because he was out with another woman. She appeared to be in her mid-twenties and apparently was a big fan of blood-red lipstick. I'm sure that she had other features, but the lips were what first caught my attention. From the way in which Toby fawned over the woman, it appeared that his interest was more than professional. I nudged Daphne. "Who's that with Toby?" I asked, indicating the woman.

Daphne looked over to where Toby was sitting. Her expression registered surprise. "Of all the ... he's out with *her*?"

"Yes, but who *is* she?" I pressed.

"Susan Henkley. She's a broker. I can't stand her."

I looked back at the woman. Once you got past the red lips, the rest of the package came into focus. She had the wiry build of someone who takes their workouts seriously. Her light brown hair hung in a pin-straight curtain halfway down her back. Her face was not unattractive; it was symmetrical with high cheekbones and a straight nose. But there was also an intensity to it that was a little off-putting. I watched as Susan leaned over and whispered something in Toby's ear. Toby laughed and put his hand on her back.

"I guess Toby doesn't share your opinion," I said.

"I guess so," Daphne agreed.

It was well after midnight when we returned to our hotel and even later than that when the phone rang. I fumbled for the light before lifting the receiver. "Hello?" I mumbled.

The voice was gruff and to the point. "Do yourself a favor," it said, "and go back to L.A. before you get your other pretty leg shot up." With that the line went dead, which was fine by me. It didn't seem like it was going to be a good conversation anyway.

"Who was that?" Nigel asked, as I turned off the light.

"*The Ladies Home Journal*," I replied. "You've been selected to receive a free trial subscription."

"Tell them no thanks," Nigel said as he pulled me close. "Their centerfolds are terrible."

EIGHTEEN

THE NEXT EVENING FOUND us at Max and Olive's apartment for their annual "Christmas Cocktail Coterie." It's almost as intolerable as its name. However, Nigel's parents, Doris and Paul, were going to be there, so Nigel and I agreed to go as well. While Paul had learned to tune out his sister, Doris could only take Olive in small doses. As a result, Doris had taken up smoking when visiting. It enabled her to politely disengage when tolerance ran out.

By the time we arrived, the party was in full swing. Joe answered our knock, his expression stoic. Behind him, the room was packed with men and women, all of a certain age, race, and income. A woman wearing a low-cut, black velvet dress was loudly singing along to Dean Martin's rendition of "Marshmallow World". It was not readily apparent why she was crying. Two men in dark suits were noisily comparing their stock options while downing martinis. Another woman was shouting into her cell phone at her children to go to sleep. My initial reaction, to quietly leave, was thwarted by the sudden appearance of Olive. She greeted me warmly; proof that the cocktail in her hand was not her first.

"Nicole!" she cried. "How lovely to see you. You should wear green more often, dear. It brings out your eyes." Turning to Nigel she said, "Nigel, dear, is it me or do you get more handsome with every passing day?"

Nigel laughed. "It's not you, darling. Don't be silly. Are my parents here?"

Olive nodded. "Your father is in there somewhere talking to Max. Your mother is out on the balcony. *Again*." Her nose crinkled with disapproval. "It's such a nasty habit. And *so* disruptive. It seems like every time we start talking, she has to duck out for a cigarette."

As Nigel went to search for his father, a task made easier with Skippy to part the crowd, I went out onto the balcony and joined Doris. In her younger days, she had studied ballet. With her tall, graceful frame, and auburn hair pulled back into a bun, she looked as if she still did. Seeing me, she smiled and waved. "Nic! Thank God. We've only been here an hour, and I'm already on my third cigarette."

"I'm supposed to tell you that it's a nasty habit."

"So is telling your sister-in-law to put a sock in it," Doris replied as she gave me a hug. "And then actually putting a sock in it for her. One of these days, I'm afraid she's going to push me too far. I actually think she's worse this year."

"I hadn't noticed," I admitted. "Isn't she always like this?"

Doris tipped her head in acknowledgment. "Well, yes. She is generally awful. But all the money problems they've had this past year have really brought out her inner crab."

I glanced around at the expensive decorations and attentive wait staff. "So, *this* is what money problems look like? It's quite disheartening when you are forced to see it up close. Do you think they'd be offended if we passed a hat around for them?"

Doris took a drag and laughed. "Well, as long as it was a hat from Chanel."

"Oh, but of course," I replied as I speared a shrimp off a passing platter.

Doris helped herself to one as well, and continued in a lower voice, "But they did have to sell one of the beach houses."

"Really? I hadn't heard that. Which one?"

"The one on Long Island," Doris said.

"Ouch. That must have hurt."

"Are you kidding? It was the jewel in Olive's crown. I believe she wore black for months afterward."

"So how did all that happen?" I asked.

Doris shrugged. "Same as it did for most people, I suppose. Housing bubble burst and money was lost." She glanced meaningfully around at the expertly decorated patio. "Of course, when certain people insist on living a certain lifestyle, the bills can add up. Speaking of those people, she tells me you bought a dog. I think I was supposed to be horrified."

"*Nigel* bought him," I corrected. "That's him right there," I added, pointing through the glass door. Doris craned her neck and peeked in.

"Christ," she said.

"Actually, his name is Skippy. Nigel claims he followed him home."

Doris shook her head. "I swear. He gets more like his father every day. I'll never forget the year Paul came home with an alpaca.

Named her Chloe. She was rather sweet, actually. Provided us some lovely sweaters."

"Where is she now?"

"A neighbor with a farm eventually took her. Paul still visits. The alpaca, that is." Turning back to me, she said, "So what's all this nonsense about Leo?"

I told her. She rolled her eyes. "Poor Audrey. Life would be so much easier if Olive didn't care so much what other people thought," she said.

"Speaking of which," I said, "where is Audrey? I thought she was supposed to be here."

"She called about an hour ago," said Doris. "She said she had a migraine or something. That boy who moons after her all the time—what's his name?"

"Toby."

"Right—Toby. Well, when he heard that she wasn't feeling well, he leapt up and ran over to her place like a good little lap dog to see if he could help."

"I take it you don't like him?"

Doris exhaled a mouthful of smoke before answering. "I wouldn't say I don't like him. I'm sure he's a perfectly respectable young man. He just seems a little … oh, what's the word?"

"Spineless?"

Doris considered it for a moment and then nodded. "That works. I mean, *really*. He and Audrey went to school together, and everyone could see that he was head over heels in love with her. But rather than propose to her or do *something*, he moves to Ohio for the year to take over some malpractice case for the firm."

"Oh, that's right. I vaguely remember Nigel telling me about that."

"It might have been a good career move, but during the year he was gone, Audrey got engaged to Leo."

"Maybe Audrey never felt that way about Toby," I said.

Doris shook her head. "No. She did. I could tell. But she's so damn insecure that she couldn't see how he felt. When he left, she figured that he never cared. Which left the door wide open for Leo."

"Who is now gone."

"Who is now gone," she agreed. "Far be it from me to tell you your business, but do you think it's wise to find him?"

I shrugged, removed the cigarette from her hand, and took a drag. "Probably not. He sounds awful. If I do find him, I reunite Audrey with a man who will eventually leave with as much of her money as he can carry. If I don't, she'll feel humiliated in front of all her friends and family. Either way, I suspect Olive will find a way to complain."

I handed the cigarette back to Doris. She inhaled one last time and then stubbed it out. "Well, look on the bright side. You're giving her an excuse to do what she loves best." Smiling, she added, "Remember, the best Christmas gifts are those that delight the recipient, not the sender."

NINETEEN

DORIS AND I WENT back inside. The woman in the black dress had stopped singing. She was still crying. Whimpering might be more accurate. In any case, it was an improvement. From what I could tell, the men in the dark suits were still comparing their stocks; however, it was loud so I may have misheard them. The woman with the non-compliant children had, thankfully, either won or given up the argument. The rest of the crowd was swilling martinis.

Nigel stood with his father. Paul was an older version of Nigel—tall, handsome, with a head of thick brown hair. Paul's hair was just starting to go gray, and his eyes were brown instead of blue, but they were surrounded by the same laugh lines. He and Nigel were talking to Max and Olive. "Hello, Mother," Nigel said to Doris as we approached. He kissed her cheek and then said, "This is Skippy." Skippy sat down, gave a sharp bark, and raised his paw.

Doris politely accepted it and shook. "Pleased to meet you, Skippy," she said.

Olive maneuvered to Doris's side. "Did you ever see such a thing?" she asked. "Only *your* son would ever think of buying such a creature, let alone bringing it *here*." She looked askance at Skippy. "God help you when these two have children. Can you imagine?"

Doris opened her mouth to respond. I quickly grabbed two flutes of champagne from a passing waiter and shoved one in Doris's empty hand. "Cheers!" I said, tapping her glass and taking a sip. Doris paused and then drained hers.

"Excuse me," she said, handing me the empty glass. "I need a cigarette."

Olive frowned. "Another one?" she called out to Doris's retreating form. "Honestly, what you need is a little self control!"

"I'm working on it as we speak," Doris called over her shoulder as she slid the balcony door shut.

Max and Daphne appeared. "Doris smoking again?" Max asked, his eyes twinkling.

Paul nodded. "It waxes and wanes."

Max smiled. "Yes. I imagine it does."

Olive opened her mouth to speak. I cut her off. "Is Audrey here tonight?" I asked in a voice I knew to be a shade too loud. Olive was predictably distracted.

"Lower your voice," she hissed. Pasting a fake smile on her face, she waved to a woman walking by. "Hello, Margie! Having fun? *Good.*" Returning her attention to us, she said in low voice, "No, she's *not.* Claims she has a headache. I don't know what I'm going to do with her. Have you had any success in finding where *he* is?"

Max turned to Paul. "I suppose you've heard that we've asked Nic here to help us with our little problem. It seems Leo has gone missing."

"Nigel was just telling me about it," said Paul. "Can't see why you'd want him back. I mean long term."

"Or short term," added Nigel.

Daphne nodded her agreement. "I, for one, don't. But if it'll help Audrey get through her party—that *some* people insisted on throwing—" she glanced meaningfully at her mother. Olive ignored her. Max chose to study the ceiling. Daphne continued, "Then I'll do whatever I can to help. She's been through enough as it is."

"And what have you found out, Nicole?" Olive now asked.

I told her about Fat Saul's death and my meeting with Frank and Danny and Lizzy. Olive looked disgusted. "You asked," I reminded her.

"So, the money that Leo owed to this Fat Saul, he now owes to Frank Little?" asked Max. "How much money are we talking about?"

"A great deal. From what Frank told me it was more than what Audrey could withdraw without your approval." I told him the amount. Max let out a string of expletives that would have made my old lieutenant proud. Olive did not appear to share the sentiment.

"Max, really," she protested. "As much as I'd like to kill the man, let's not be vulgar."

For Olive, it didn't matter what the message was as long as it was said with an air of class.

"And he was having an affair with this Lizzy woman?" Max asked, ignoring Olive.

I shrugged. "That I don't know. She said they were just friends. But I suspect her definition of 'friends' might be broader than most."

"What does she look like?" asked Olive.

"Very tan, very blonde, very everything," I said.

Nigel expanded the description. "Rode hard and put away dirty."

Daphne laughed. "I believe the expression is 'rode hard and put away wet.'"

Nigel shrugged. "You say tomato; I say prostitute."

"Well, in any case, I don't think we should mention any of this to Audrey," I said. "I think there is more going on with this woman than she's saying. Until I find out what that is, I don't think we should mention it to her. It'll only further upset her."

Doris returned. "Upset who?" she asked.

Olive sniffed. "Maybe if you'd stop smoking, you wouldn't miss so much."

Doris smiled. "Oh, of that I'm certain."

"We were just talking about Audrey," Nigel explained. "Nic got a lead on Leo. We found a woman who is a kind of friend of his, but they don't want to tell Audrey just yet. No use getting her hopes up."

"Or down, as the case may be," Doris said. "If Audrey's father were alive today, there would be no Leo problem." She paused and considered. "Actually, there probably would be no *Leo*. David didn't put up with his kind."

Max smiled. "To absent friends," he said, raising his glass.

"To absent friends," we repeated in kind.

TWENTY

By MIDNIGHT, I WAS ready to take up smoking, and the waiter and I were on a first-name basis. It was past time to go home. I found Nigel talking to Daphne and a colorless woman I didn't remember. Seeing me, she grabbed both of my hands and cooed, "Nicole! Why, look at you! And in a dress! Marriage certainly agrees with you! You look so feminine!" I guessed her to be a close friend of Olive's.

I debated telling her that my newly feminine look was more due to hormone therapy than marital bliss, but frankly, I was too tired. I wanted my bed. Nigel frowned at the woman. "Too bad the same can't be said for every woman," he said after giving her a long look. Turning to me, he said, "It's time to go home, dear. Where's Skippy?"

Skippy was chewing on something in the corner. I fished what I could out of his mouth. Most of it appeared to be discarded paperwork, mostly receipts: grocery, catering, wine, work licenses, as well as some confetti and toilet paper. What bits I couldn't retrieve, I left for nature to handle. Nigel and I said our good-byes and left.

The next day was Christmas Eve. Nigel woke me at dawn to ask if I wanted my present. "Unless it's four more hours of sleep, then no," I replied before shoving my head back under the pillow.

"But they're getting restless," Nigel protested. "And when that happens they start to shed."

I cut him off. "Nigel, it's not Christmas yet."

He pushed his head into my neck. "Please?"

I sighed. "If I give you your present now, will you let me go back to sleep?"

"Yes," he said, bouncing the bed with excitement. "I'll get yours. I was just kidding about them getting restless before."

"I would hope so," I said as I sat up and wiped the sleep from my eyes.

"Yeah, they're already dead."

"Perfect." Nigel placed a Bellini in my hand. I looked at it in confusion. "This isn't a Christmas present, Nigel, it's breakfast."

"I know. Wait a second." He pulled a small box out of the closet and placed it on my lap. I lifted the top and looked inside. "Thank you, Nigel! It's beautiful!" I said, lifting out the double-strand pearl necklace. "Yours is under the bed."

"I know," Nigel said as he jumped off the bed and peered underneath it. "I found it yesterday, but I didn't peek." He ripped off the wrappings, opened the box, and pulled out the watch he'd been mooning over for the past few months. Kissing me soundly on the lips, he said, "Thank you, darling. I love you. Merry Christmas."

"I love you, too, dear. Can we go back to sleep now?"

"Wait, we have to give Skippy his presents."

"I hadn't realized that we'd gotten Skippy presents," I admitted.

"I know. I signed your name to the card anyway," he said as he grabbed a bag off the closet shelf. Skippy wagged his tail excitedly and let out a happy bark. Nigel pulled out a stuffed snowman and tossed it in the air. Skippy leapt up and caught the toy in his mouth. It let out a loud squeak.

Nigel crawled back into bed with me. Random squeaking sounds pierced the air. I curled up next to Nigel. "You didn't know that it made a noise, did you?" I asked.

"There's a distinct possibility I overlooked that fact."

After we removed the snowman's squeaker, we went back to sleep. When we awoke again at a more civilized hour, we had breakfast sent up. Afterward, we opted to stay in our hotel room. We were due to meet Nigel's entire family for six o'clock mass at St. Patrick's, but until then we saw no reason to venture outside. There, it was cold, windy, and filled with Martinis. And not the good kind. As Nigel said, you had to pace yourself with Martinis. Our bodies were far too fragile for the demands they put upon them. Instead, we spent the majority of the day engaged in far more enjoyable pursuits.

By four it was time to get ready. "Come on, Nigel," I said when I stepped out of the shower. "We need to get a move on, or we'll be late."

Nigel was sprawled on the couch nursing his Dirty Martini and reading the paper. "But what about Skippy?" he asked. Skippy who was lying calmly at Nigel's feet, perked his ears up attentively at the sound of his name. "We can't leave him alone on Christmas Eve."

"I don't think he's a practicing Christian. He'll be fine. Besides, I've arranged for one of the more tolerant members of the hotel staff to look in on him."

Nigel was unconvinced. "Do we really have to go?" he asked glancing at the blustering sky outside.

"Yes," I replied. "It's Christmas. We're going to church."

"*This* is my church," he said, nodding respectfully to his Dirty Martini.

Resting my hand on his shoulder, I said, "Darling, this is one of those red flags we read about. Step away from the cocktail, and get your ass ready for church."

By some form of divine intervention, which came in the form of finding an available cab, we arrived at St. Patrick's in time to find a seat near the rest of the family. Olive, with her fur coat slung over her shoulders like a poncho, smiled and gave us a half wave as if she were a queen receiving visitors.

I slid into the pew next to Doris and Paul. "Merry almost Christmas," I said. "How are you?"

"Better now that Olive has taken her pills," Doris replied, casing an irritated glance in Olive's direction. "She was livid at the potential scandal of Leo not attending mass with the family. Threw a monster of a fit."

I looked over to where Audrey sat. She was one down from Olive, next to Max. She looked very pale and delicate. Her blonde hair was tucked neatly under a black velvet hat. "How is Audrey holding up?" I asked.

"She's trying to keep it together, but it can't be easy with Olive wailing about it every five minutes," she said.

"No, I imagine not," I said as the choir began to sing, signaling the start of mass.

———

When mass was over, we filed out into the cold night and made our way to Max and Olive's. Once inside, Max took my coat. "Joe has the night off, I take it?" I asked.

Max smiled. "It wasn't without a fight, I assure you."

"You're kidding?" I said in surprise. "Olive really wanted Joe to work on Christmas Eve?"

Max shook his head. "No, it was the other way around. Joe wanted to help out. Very thoughtful of him, but it's a little too Ebenezer for my taste."

"I have to say that is surprising. Joe must have changed since when I knew him."

Max laughed and said, "Speaking of which, one of these days you'll have to tell me about our esteemed butler's former life. I have the distinct impression that Janet Harris had a bit of fun at our expense."

Before I could answer, Olive descended upon us. "Nicole! Nigel!" she cooed. "Merry Christmas! Wasn't it a lovely service? I so enjoy St. Patrick's. They do know how to put on a Christmas mass."

"You make it sound like a play, darling," Nigel said as he leaned in to kiss her.

"Don't be blasphemous," she admonished. Noticing my pearl necklace, she added, "What a lovely necklace, Nicole. Is it new?"

"Yes," I said as I raised my hand to touch the pearls. "Nigel gave it to me for Christmas."

Olive frowned. "But it's not Christmas yet! And besides, I specifically told you to get Nicole a fur coat, Nigel. After all, she's a Martini now. You have a societal duty."

"I know, dear. And I take medication for it." With a wink, he added, "I'll get my second wife a fur coat."

I elbowed him in the ribs. "I'd like to see you live that long."

Olive let out a frustrated sigh and declared Nigel "impossible." His mission accomplished, Nigel led me to the living room to join the rest of the family.

Daphne was standing with Audrey and Toby by the bar. Nigel busied himself making us a drink while I said hello to everyone. "What was Mother crabbing at you for this time?" Daphne asked me.

"We've scandalized her by exchanging our Christmas presents a day early," I answered.

"What heathens you are," she said, laughing.

Nigel handed me my drink. "So, what are your plans for tomorrow?" Daphne asked us.

"We are taking Nigel's parents to Radio City to see the Rockettes's Christmas show," I answered.

Daphne looked at Nigel in surprise. "Seriously? You're going to see the Rockettes?" she asked.

Nigel nodded. "I've never been. If I'm going to be in New York for Christmas, then I'm going to do every cliché thing I can. After the show, we are going skating at Rockefeller Center and then buy some hot chocolate and take a stroll up Fifth Avenue and look at the windows at Bergdorf Goodman."

Daphne laughed and shook her head. "You two will be a walking brochure for New York by the time you're through."

"What are your plans?" I asked.

Daphne shrugged. "Nothing nearly as fun. I'm bringing Audrey over in the morning, and we'll exchange gifts and have dinner. I don't expect it to be a particular jolly day. Now that I think about it, I may have to go into the office."

Nigel sputtered. "On Christmas? You're kidding, right? Why would you need to go into the office on Christmas?"

Daphne produced a grim smile. "I don't believe that I said I 'need' to go into the office. I said I 'may' have to. And after a few hours here, you might find yourself longing for the peace and quiet of an empty office too."

We all looked over to where Olive stood talking to Audrey. She appeared to be lecturing her. Audrey stood meekly, her head hung low.

"I stand corrected," said Nigel. "If I were you, I might even stop off somewhere and donate blood."

"Nigel," I said with a laugh, "After this week, the only thing your blood would be good for would be pickling."

"Well, we all need a talent," he said.

———

Nigel and I spent Christmas day as planned. We met up with Doris and Paul and spent the day playing tourist, complete with window-shopping, drinking hot cocoa, skating, and watching the Rockettes. It was nice not to concentrate on missing philanders, critical in-laws, and truculent ex-cons. Of course, it didn't last. It never does.

———

I awoke the next morning to the phone ringing. Nigel raised his head off the pillow and cast a baleful eye at it. "Every time I hear that phone, it's ringing," he complained before returning to sleep. I fumbled for the receiver. The nightstand clock read 7:00 a.m.

"You've reached the body of Nic Martini," I said. "Please leave a message."

"Nic?" said a voice. It sounded far away. "Are you there?"

"In a metaphysical sense," I admitted. "Who is this?"

"Marcy. Did I wake you? Look, I'm sorry to bother you," she went on without waiting for my answer, "but something's come up."

I yawned. "Such as?"

"That woman who was seeing Leo? Lizzy Marks? Well, she's dead. And in case you're wondering, it wasn't natural causes."

I sighed. "No. It wouldn't be, would it?"

TWENTY-ONE

ACCORDING TO MARCY, LIZZY had been killed sometime late Christmas night. She'd been found by a neighbor who'd become concerned when she'd noticed the apartment door wide open. "She was a door-shut kind of lady, if you know what I mean," the neighbor had explained. Marcy said she did.

There was no sign of forced entry, so the police were working on the assumption that she knew her killer. From what I knew about Lizzy, that didn't exactly narrow the field. It was assumed that Lizzy had not been expecting a romantic visit based on her outfit: workout clothes. While they were spandex and left little to the imagination, Marcy said it appeared that Lizzy had recently been exercising. There was a workout video in the DVD player, and there were free weights nearby. The coroner concluded that Lizzy died from an impact to the head by a blunt object. She'd fallen—or been pushed—onto the kidney-shaped table I'd seen when I'd visited.

"Do you think your friend Leo could have had anything to do with this?" Marcy asked me.

I sat up in the bed and answered. "A: He's not my friend, and B: I have no idea. It would be nice in a way if he did. It would be the simplest way to get him out of Audrey's life. But from what I know about Leo, if he killed every woman he had an affair with, there'd be a hell of a lot more bodies piled up."

"You make a valid point. However, I was thinking about that call to Fat Saul before he went out and got himself shot."

"You think Lizzy might have made that call?" I asked.

"At the very least, it's a possibility. However, it could be that someone just wants us to think that she did."

"And by 'someone' do you mean Frank Little?"

"I might."

"But for what reason? Why would Frank want to kill Lizzy?"

"That I can't answer. But you said yourself that there's a lot of money involved here. I just feel like I'm missing a piece of the puzzle."

"I think that piece might be Leo."

"Which is why we're looking for him. I assume that you'll let me know if you hear of anything?" she asked.

"Wait, now that I think of it, Frank mentioned something about Lizzy having an ex-husband who wasn't taking the divorce very well. Thought he could beat her into changing her mind."

"Who says romance is dead?" she said. "Any idea what this Romeo's name is?"

I rubbed my eyes. "Billy something. Billy Morgan."

"Right. Well, thanks for the tip. I'll let you know if I find anything and vice versa."

"You'll be the first one I call," I assured her.

After I hung up the phone, I turned to Nigel. "That was Marcy. Lizzy Marks is dead. She was found this morning. Hit her head on the table."

"Dear God," he said his eyes wide. "Did Marcy say if they know who did it?"

I shook my head. "Not yet. No sign of forced entry, but they don't think she was expecting company. She was in her workout clothes."

"I think she was in those when we paid her a visit."

"Point taken."

Nigel frowned. "I don't like the idea of you being involved with this. Finding a missing husband is one thing; murder is something very different."

"Don't worry about me," I said with a smile. "I'm in no danger."

"Maybe. But I want to keep it that way," he said.

I leaned over and kissed him. "I promise I'll be safe. Anyway, Marcy would very much like to talk to Leo."

Nigel sat up and pushed the bed covers aside. "Wouldn't we all? But why would Leo kill Lizzy?" he asked.

I shrugged. "Who knows? But according to Frank, Fat Saul received a phone call from a woman before he went out. Maybe Lizzy did know where Leo was and called Fat Saul. Maybe Lizzy wasn't as loyal to Leo as she claimed."

"So, Leo kills Fat Saul and then figures out that Lizzy was the one who ratted him out, so he kills her too?" Nigel asked as he glanced over the room service menu. "I want coffee. And eggs. And then more coffee." He put the menu down and sighed. "Seems a little too simple."

"Throw in some bacon and a bread basket."

"I meant about Leo. But you make a valid suggestion."

———

Marcy called me later that morning to tell me that they had picked up Lizzy's ex-husband, Billy Morgan, for questioning. "He's a real charmer," Marcy said. "I think you'll like him."

"Is that an invitation to come to the station?" I asked.

"I guess so. I can think of at least ten different places I'd rather be, but we can't all have the same idea as to how to spend an afternoon in New York."

"Thanks, Marcy. I'll be right there."

I left Nigel and Skippy curled up on the bed watching *A Christmas Story*. Outside, it was cold and windy. The sky was an ominous shade of dark gray. I pulled my coat tightly against me and asked the bellman to hail me a cab. It took him several minutes to find one. I gave the doorman a generous tip for his trouble and directed the cab driver to take me to the 76th Precinct in Brooklyn. It had been a few years since I'd been there, but the building was unchanged. It was your standard government structure, made of cement and brick. The fact that it housed criminals might also be considered by some to be a standard government feature.

Marcy met me at the front desk, signed me in, and handed me a temporary badge. I followed her down the hall to an interrogation room. Inside was a long metal table and a few chairs. At the table sat the man I'd seen smoking outside of Lizzy's apartment. He had a muscular build and almost no neck. He glanced up when I entered but didn't appear to recognize me.

"Who's she?" he asked Marcy in a gravely voice as she pulled out a chair and sat down.

"A concerned citizen," Marcy answered. "Now, why don't you tell me about your relationship with your ex-wife."

"Well, considering that she was my *ex-wife*, I guess you could say that it wasn't too good," he sneered.

"You're not too clever are you, Billy?" Marcy asked. "Your ex-wife ends up dead, apparently as the result of some altercation, and you want to make jokes about how you didn't get along?"

Billy pushed back in his chair. "I'm not going to lie to you. I hated her. She double crossed me. When I got sent to jail, she divorced me and stole my money."

"What money was this?" Marcy asked.

"It was from an insurance scam. I got busted and she got the money. When I got out I paid her a visit to remind her that she owed me."

Marcy opened a file on the table in front of her and pulled out a paper. "Oh, yes. I think I have a record of that visit. Would this be the visit during which you broke her arm?"

Billy frowned. "You can't prove that was me."

"And yet your ex-wife did just that—got a restraining order against you too. How far away were you supposed to stay?" Marcy asked.

"Five hundred feet. And I did, too."

Marcy put the paper back into the folder. "And yet we have witnesses who claim that they saw you outside her apartment on several occasions."

"I might have been in the neighborhood," Billy admitted. "But I never got closer than five hundred feet."

"Well, that remains to be seen," said Marcy. "Why don't you tell me what you know about her? Any idea what she was doing?"

Billy shrugged. "Not really, but I knew she was working some kind of scam. She'd got herself a real job at some office. She was smart, I'll give her that. She could get anyone's confidence. Look, I didn't kill her. I swear. I just wanted her to pay me back my money. That's all I wanted."

"From the sound of it, you were outside her apartment a fair amount of time. Did you see anything suspicious?" Marcy asked.

Billy shook his head. "No. People going in and out."

Marcy tapped the folder with her fingernail. "You must have started to recognize the people who lived in the building. Did you see anyone new?"

Billy furrowed his forehead in concentration. "There were a few people. Saw a couple with a crazy big dog."

Marcy glanced at me. "Uh-huh. We know about them. Anyone else?"

Billy thought some more, but was of no real help. It seems that Lizzy's building had many visitors. He'd seen an uptight blonde, a dumpy grandmother, a maintenance man, and a thin man with slick hair. This last one might have been Leo, but it was too vague to prove anything.

"Did you know that she was planning on leaving?" Marcy asked.

Billy looked at her in confusion. "She was leaving?" he repeated.

Marcy nodded. "Sure looked that way. Her suitcases were packed. Any idea on where she was going?"

Billy shook his head. "No idea. Honestly. I didn't know that."

I found myself believing him. Which really ticked me off. It would be so much easier if Billy had killed Lizzy.

———

That evening, we were due to join Daphne, Olive, Max, and Nigel's parents at an art exhibit downtown. It was a celebration of expensive blurry French landscapes, expensive abstract still lifes, and, for good measure, a few expensive nudes. The nudes were—typically—solely female. By the time we arrived, the room was packed with art lovers of all varieties. They ranged from true aficionados to pontificating pseudo-intellectuals. Nigel and I found ourselves behind the latter. She was standing in front of a painting depicting a table, a jug of water, and a plate of cheese and bread.

"As you can see," the woman said to her husband, "in this piece, the artist is attempting to portray the suffering of the working class poor through the juxtaposition of the cheese and bread."

Her husband squinted at the painting. "He is?"

"Of course. Here, let me show you." She put her arm around him and leaned in close. With her free hand, she gestured at the painting. "The jug represents the upper class. As you can see, it's larger and in the foreground, while the bread and cheese is pushed to the back."

"You sure know a lot about art," Nigel remarked loudly.

The woman turned to us in surprise. "Why, Nigel! Hello, dear! I didn't see you there. Hello, Nicole," she added.

"Hello, Olive," I replied. "Hi, Max."

Max winked at me. "Olive was just enlightening me on the meaning of this picture," he said.

"Painting, dear," Olive corrected.

Nigel nodded solemnly. "Yes, I heard, and I agree with you, Aunt Olive. There is a message in this painting. It's not immediately apparent, of course. Only one truly versed in the language of art would see it."

Olive glanced back at the painting and then at Nigel. "So you agree with me then?" she asked. "About the suffering of the working class?"

"Hmm? Oh, God no." said Nigel. "It has a totally different meaning. Look at it again. Jug of water. Plate of bread and cheese. What strikes you, Nic?"

"No meat," I said.

"Exactly," beamed Nigel. "Where's the meat? That's the message. Speaking of which, I'm hungry. Let's see if they have any snacks here."

We walked away before Olive could chastize us and found Nigel's parents. They were staring morosely at the food table. "This isn't food," Paul complained, indicating the spread of celery, carrots, olives, and other vegan staples. "It's *toppings* for food. But there's no food to top."

"It's a crudité platter, dear," explained Doris. "It's supposed to be healthy."

"Then why is there a fully stocked bar?" countered Paul. "Are you going to tell me that scotch is healthy?"

"Of course not," replied Nigel. "But how else do you expect to get the celery down?"

"My goodness, there are so many wonderful paintings here!" Olive said as she rejoined us. "I wish I had more walls at home! Hello, Doris. Hello, Paul," she continued brightly. "Aren't you all having the best time? Oh, what an elegant table! Max, be a dear and fix me a veggie plate. I'm famished. Buying art always has that effect on me."

Turning to Doris, Olive said, "I've bought six paintings so far. Can you believe it? Six! But you know me. You'd be hard pressed to find a bigger art lover than me."

"Or a bigger..." began Doris. Paul quickly handed her a celery stick. She took it and commenced chewing.

"See that painting over there?" Olive asked, indicating a lethargic nude in the bathtub. "I bought it."

Doris turned and looked. She quickly took another bite of celery.

"It's quite..." Paul said before trailing off into a dumfounded silence.

"Isn't it?" Olive agreed excitedly. "Anyway, I'm not sure if I have room for it right now. Would you like it for your house?"

Doris coughed on her celery. I politely slapped her on her back. Paul shook his head. "That's very kind of you," he said. "No."

"But Paul," Olive began. She was interrupted by the arrival of Toby and Daphne. Daphne was just ending a phone call. She looked tired and frazzled. Toby's expression was more somber than usual.

"Hello," Daphne said to us. "Have any of you heard from Audrey? She was supposed to meet me here, and she's not answering her phone."

No one had. "Well, I'm sure she'll be here," said Olive. "But while we're on the subject, is there any news about Leo? I don't think I need to remind you, Nicole, that the party is tomorrow."

She didn't. And yet she did it anyway.

"I still don't know where Leo is," I said. "But I do have news."

I quickly told them that Lizzy Marks had been found dead, and the police suspected foul play.

"What do you mean they 'suspect' foul play? Isn't it obvious? Leo killed her," said Daphne.

"Why do you think Leo killed her?" Toby asked.

Daphne stumbled over her answer. "Well, obviously I don't know for *sure*. But Nic said that they were having an affair. Maybe they had a falling out or something."

"I never said it was certain that they were having an affair," I protested.

Daphne rolled her eyes. "Don't be naïve. Of course they were having an affair. Why else would Leo be with a woman like that? The scintillating conversation?"

"I'll admit it's the most likely possibility," I agreed. "The night Fat Saul was shot, he was out looking for Leo. According to Frank, a woman called Fat Saul with some information as to where Leo might be hiding."

"This Lizzy person!" said Daphne.

"Maybe. The police don't know yet. And, as of now they aren't saying anything with regard to a suspect. At least not to me, anyway."

Daphne stared at me in confusion. "But ..."

Olive cut her off. "Oh, dear God. What will the press do with this? Is there any way we can keep it out of the papers? This will kill Audrey." She opened her purse and began to rummage through it. "Where are my pills? I feel another anxiety attack coming on." She quickly flipped open the bottle cap and tossed two white pills down her throat. Chasing it down with a gulp of wine, she then turned to me and asked, "What do you plan to do about this, Nicole?"

I stared at her in confusion. "What do I plan to do about what?"

Olive took a deep breath and spoke as one might to a child. "About minimizing the publicity, of course. Can't you talk to your police friends and make them understand that Audrey has suffered enough? To have her see the sordid details of Leo's latest betrayal splashed across every tabloid is too much to ask of the poor child."

"Your estimation of my influence flatters me. And that's not something I ever thought I'd say. But I have no control over what the police or the press do. Besides, Audrey was bound to find out about their relationship eventually. Just thank God that she didn't know about Lizzy earlier. The police would definitely have some uncomfortable questions for her otherwise. "

An awkward silence met my remark. "No one told Audrey about Lizzy, right?" I asked.

Daphne glanced at Olive. Olive pressed her lips together and stuck out her chin. "Well, what if I did?" she said. "After all, I think she has a right to know what her husband is doing."

My left temple throbbed. "You told her about Lizzy?" I snapped. "Why? I *specifically* told you not to! You *specifically* agreed not to!"

"She needed to know the truth about him," Olive began.

"She knew the truth about him!" I countered. "She didn't care! But now the police are going to want to talk to her!"

Olive bristled. "That's ridiculous. Why would they want to talk to Audrey? She didn't have anything to do with that woman's death."

"How do you know?" I asked. "Were you there?"

"Of course not!" Olive said dismissively. "I just know Audrey. She wouldn't hurt a fly. The only crime Audrey ever committed was marrying Leo."

"Well, given her absurd devotion to him, she might be all the more upset at the woman who possibly ratted him out to Fat Saul."

Olive sniffed. "You know I don't understand that rough jargon. Please speak English."

"Gladly. You're an idiot. Now, if you'll excuse me, I've got to find Audrey and talk to her before the police do."

TWENTY-TWO

THE FACT THAT AUDREY wasn't answering Daphne's phone calls didn't necessarily mean she wasn't at home. Happy to have an excuse to leave the art show, Nigel and I made our way to Audrey's apartment. It was a sprawling, five-bedroom, three-fireplace dwelling in one of New York's most sought-after locales. Luckily, the guard at the front desk knew Nigel and waved us upstairs. Outside Audrey's door, our repeated knocks went unanswered. However, I swore I heard faint movement inside, so we persisted. Finally, Nigel called out, "Audrey? Please open up. It's about Leo. There's been an accident. He's in the hospital, and he's calling for you."

Within seconds the door swung open. I quickly stepped inside the large foyer before she could rethink her decision. Audrey's face was puffy from crying. Her hair was disheveled, her nose was red, and I smelled alcohol on her breath. "Leo's calling for me?" she asked, her voice wobbly, her eyes fearful.

"How should I know?" Nigel answered good-naturedly as he let Skippy off his leash. Skippy gave a happy bark and ran off.

"Wait," said Audrey slowly. "So, Leo isn't in the hospital?" Her voice steadied, but the fear in her eyes remained.

Nigel sighed. "It's called a lie, Audrey. Do yourself a favor and don't drink your feelings anymore tonight. I have no idea if Leo is hurt or if he's even calling for you. However, if I had to guess, I'd guess no. Now where's the bottle?"

"What bottle?"

Nigel rolled his eyes. "The bottle containing whatever it is you're drinking."

"Oh. In the kitchen."

"Thank you. Next, do you have any coffee? I'm going to make you a pot."

"Um, yes. That's in the kitchen, too."

Nigel nodded. "Then, unless you ladies need me, I will be in the kitchen."

I turned to Audrey. She stared back at me miserable, tipsy, and confused. "What's going on? Is Leo in trouble? Is he … is he in jail?"

I steered her into the living room. "I don't know," I answered. "Should he be?"

"No … I mean, I don't think so. No, of course not."

"That's reassuring," I said as I gently pushed her down onto a black suede couch. Behind it was a mahogany console table crowded with silver-framed pictures of Audrey and Leo, and a silver bowl filled with Werther's caramels. I sat down in a gray-and-cream striped wingback chair. On the coffee table between us was another silver bowl filled with more Werther's caramels. "What's with all the candy?" I asked.

Audrey looked down at the bowl of candy. Her lower lip trembled. "Those are Leo's favorites. I keep them around the house for him."

I restrained myself from asking if Leo was a six-year-old who could be bribed with sweets. "Okay. Listen, I need to ask you something, Audrey. And I need you to be honest."

Audrey's gaze slid away from mine and focused on the chair next to me. "Okay."

"Did you go to Lizzy Marks's apartment?"

"Whose apartment?"

"Please don't play dumb with me. I'm in no mood. I'm tired, and I have a headache. I know that Olive told you about Lizzy Marks. What I need to know is whether or not you went to her apartment."

"No, no, of course not," Audrey told the chair. "Why would I do that?"

"Because you knew Leo was involved with her," I answered.

Audrey squeezed her eyes shut. "That's ... that's not true. You don't know that. Who told you that?"

"Lizzy, actually. She told me when I went to see her a few days ago."

Audrey's eyes flew open, and she looked at me. "Was Leo there?"

"No."

"What ... what did she tell you? Did she say whether she was ... did she know where Leo was?"

I helped myself to a Werther's and leaned back into the chair. "She claimed not to know where Leo was. As for the rest, well, she said a lot of things. Who knows if any of it was true?"

"Was she in love with him?"

"Does it matter?" I asked, popping the candy in my mouth.

"I don't know. It might." She stared at me for a moment, seeming to debate something.

"Leo owed a lot of money to a man named Fat Saul. Ever hear of him?"

Audrey shook her head. "No. I only heard him talk about Frank. Frank Little."

"Yes, I know. Frank worked for Fat Saul. Apparently, Fat Saul wanted Leo to pay back the entire loan."

Audrey opened her mouth, no doubt to protest that she always covered Leo's debts, but I cut her off. "It was more than what you could take out without Max and Olive co-signing," I said. Audrey flinched as if I'd slapped her. "Once Fat Saul called in the loan, Leo dropped out of sight."

"So you think that's why Leo's gone?"

"It's a possibility. However, the other night someone killed Fat Saul. We know that the night he died, he got a call from a woman and then went out looking for Leo."

Audrey's eyes grew wide. "Are you saying that Leo had something to do with that man's death?"

I shook my head. "No. I'm only telling you what happened. But it is a possibility. If Fat Saul found out where Leo was hiding, and went there, there might have been a fight. It's possible that Leo killed Fat Saul in self-defense."

Audrey stared at me. "Do you think that's what happened?"

"I have no idea."

Audrey closed her eyes and sank back into the couch. "Oh, God. Where is he?" she moaned.

"That does seem to be the sixty-four thousand dollar question. However, that's not why I'm here. I need to know if you went to Lizzy's. The truth."

Nigel came into the room carrying a tray. Setting it down on the oval coffee table, he handed Audrey a cup of coffee. "Drink this," he instructed.

Audrey took a sip. Nigel poured me a cup and passed it to me. From somewhere in the house came the sound of something falling over and nails skidding on a wood floor. "What was that?" Audrey asked.

"Reindeer," said Nigel. "I believe Nic was asking you something?"

Audrey took another sip. Then another.

"Audrey," I said after her third sip, "I already know Olive told you all about Lizzy. What I need to know now is if you went there."

"But why?"

"Because she's dead," I said gauging her reaction to this news. Audrey didn't appear shocked. "And when—not if—the police find out that you knew about her, they're going to want to question you. And they won't be as nice as me. So, for the last time, Audrey, tell me what happened."

Audrey took a deep breath and burst into tears. "I didn't kill her," she sobbed. "I swear! She was already dead when I got there! Oh God! What have I done?"

TWENTY-THREE

IT TOOK SEVERAL MINUTES to get a coherent story out of Audrey. Finally, she told us that after Olive told her about Lizzy, she'd gone home and tried to calm down. "But I was just too mad," she said, once her tears had subsided. "Why was he with her of all people? I'd given him everything! Everything! And he humiliates me by going off with *her*! He *promised* he would stop. After Aunt Olive told me about her, I figured that that's where he'd been holed up. I decided to go there and tell him what I thought of him. When I got there, I saw that the door was open. I knocked, but there was no answer. So I . . . I walked in. That's when I saw her. She was lying on the floor. I knew she was dead. Her eyes . . ." Audrey closed her own eyes at the memory. After a minute, she continued. "I know I should have called the police, but I just wanted to get away from there. I had to get away from her eyes."

"What time was this?" I asked.

"About eleven-thirty."

"Did you see anything that might have indicated that Leo had been there?"

"No. Absolutely not," she said immediately.

"Take your time. No need to rush your answer."

She took a deep breath. "I didn't see anything. I just saw her. And then I left."

"Did anyone see you there?" I asked.

"No, I was careful not to let anyone see me," she said with a hint of pride.

I sighed. "Actually, it would have been better had you been seen. The police think Lizzy was killed earlier in the evening."

Audrey stared at me, her eyes wide. "I don't understand."

"Yes. That much I know," I said.

From the other room came the sound of crashing glass. Nigel put his cup on the table and stood up. "Excuse me for moment," he said before heading toward the chaos in the other room.

Audrey and I sat in silence listening to Nigel try to coax Skippy back onto his leash. Audrey sat quietly and picked at her nails. "Audrey, if you know something, you really need to tell me," I said.

Audrey continued to stare at her hands. "I've told you everything," she said, her voice small.

I took a sip of my coffee. I didn't believe her for one second.

After Nigel got Skippy onto his leash, I called Daphne and told her what had happened. "Balls," she said, her voice annoyed. "The little idiot."

"I agree. But she's in no condition to be left alone. Can you come over?"

"I'll see what I can do. I just got a call from one of my clients and have to take care of something for them. If I can't come, then I'll send Toby."

"Fine. We'll wait until one of you shows up."

"Okay. Bye."

———

Toby arrived twenty minutes later. "What's happened?" he asked as he shrugged out of his overcoat.

"When Audrey heard that Leo was seeing Lizzy Marks, she decided to pay her a visit. Unfortunately, when Audrey got there, Lizzy was dead."

Toby's brown eyes grew wide. "That's not good."

"That's putting it mildly. She tried to drown out the experience with scotch. We made her some coffee, and Nigel took away the scotch..."

"A good start."

"But I think someone should be with her tonight. To put it mildly, she's a mess."

Toby shook his head. "The poor thing. She doesn't deserve this. Don't worry. I'll take care of her. I'll make sure she's okay."

"That's good, but there's more. Audrey found the woman dead, but she didn't call the police. She just left."

Toby shook his head. "Oh, Audrey," he said under his breath.

"Yeah. Well, I think you'll agree that this is a problem. She left a crime scene and neglected to call anyone. She needs to rectify that."

Toby looked at me, his expression guarded. "What are you suggesting?"

I blinked. "Wow. Okay. I didn't think I was being unclear. I'll try again." I took a deep breath. "She needs to pick up a phone and call the police and tell them what she knows. Did you get my meaning that time?"

From the shocked look on Toby's face, I gathered he did. "Are you crazy?" he hissed. "Can you imagine the field day the press would have if they got ahold of this? They'd crucify her!"

I stared back at Toby in equal disbelief. "Do you have any idea what the police will do to her once they find out that she was at the apartment of her husband's lover? And that she found the woman dead and *did nothing*? What the press would do to her pales in comparison to what the police will do!"

Toby shook his head. "I understand your concern, Nic. I do. But Audrey was under no obligation to report anything to the police. I would think as a former detective, you'd know that."

"Yes, legally she doesn't have to. But what about her moral obligation? What about what a prosecutor will do with those facts if it comes out? Because, let's be honest. It will come out."

Toby bristled. "Not if I can help it. She's been through enough. I will not let her suffer anymore."

"If she calls the police now and tells them, she won't suffer. But if she doesn't, it will only be worse for her."

"I disagree and as her lawyer, I will advise her not to talk to the police about this. And, I'd advise you to do the same." I stared back at Toby in disbelief. He had suddenly morphed into someone quite different. Doris would never think to call the steely-eyed stone-faced man in front of me now "spineless."

"You're making a mistake, Toby," I said. "But Audrey will be the one to pay for that mistake. Is that what you want?"

"Of course not," said Toby. "I only want to take care of her and protect her. That's all I've ever wanted to do."

Remembering his cozy date the other night, I wondered if that was still true.

———

Nigel and I left a few minutes later. Audrey was slumped in Toby's arms. Despite the lousy circumstances, she looked happier than I'd seen her all week.

"Why do I have this nagging suspicion that Olive will still find a way to blame me when this all hits the fan?" I asked.

Nigel wrapped a comforting arm around my shoulder. "Don't take this the wrong way, darling, but if you only have a 'nagging' suspicion that Aunt Olive is going to blame you, then maybe it was a good thing after all that you got shot and had to quit the department. You must have been a crummy detective."

"Thanks."

"Anytime. Are you going to call Marcy?"

"Toby asked me not to. I think I agreed," I said.

"Well, to hand Audrey to the police now would be akin to kicking a puppy. I think you can give yourself a break on this one."

"I wonder if Marcy would agree. I have a headache from this case," I complained. "I need a hot bath and then a dirty martini."

"Your wish is my command," Nigel said offering me his arm. "And, if you're a very good girl, I'll take you out for a drink afterwards."

Before I could answer, my phone rang. According to the readout, it was from either Max or Olive. I looked at it in dismay. "I think this is your Aunt Olive calling," I said.

"Oh, well," said Nigel. "Better to rip off the Band-Aid than to let it linger."

"Gee, that's comforting." I answered the phone with a lukewarm greeting, while I mentally steeled myself to do battle with Olive.

"Hey, Detective Landis...I mean, Mrs. Martini," said a deep voice. "This is Jo...seph."

"Why, hello Joe," I answered, looking at Nigel in surprise. "What can I do for you?"

"Well, I thought you'd like to know something. I know where that scumbag Leo is. I just saw him at a club I go to sometimes. He's in there throwing around money like it grows on trees."

"Technically, it does," I said.

"Huh? Oh. Yeah. Well, anyway, I thought I'd let you know. So, we're good, right? You're not going to tell Mrs. Beasley about my past, right?"

"I wouldn't dream of it," I said with true honesty. "Speaking of which, are they home yet?"

"No. I had to stop in to deliver some things for Mrs. Beasley. I thought I'd call you while I was here."

"I appreciate that Joe. What's the name of the club?"

"It's The Lucky Lady. It's on 83rd and Broadway."

"Thanks, Joe. But enlighten me, why are you telling me this? You know as well as I do that Frank Little has put a bounty out on Leo's head. You could have called Frank and made some money in the process."

There was a brief pause. "Yeah, I know. But I know how much it means to Miss Audrey to have Leo at her party. She's a nice kid. She don't deserve this. I figured Frank could wait one more day before getting his hands on Leo. But it seemed a shame to ruin Miss Audrey's party."

"You're a regular softie, Joe. Thanks. I'll check it out." I hung up and told Nigel.

"The Lucky Lady?" he repeated. "Let me guess; it's listed in the phonebook under 'I' for irony."

Traffic being its usual fickle self, it was some time later before we arrived at the club. The Lucky Lady was housed in a nondescript kind of building. Shuttered windows. Peeling paint. A heavy steel door. The only bright spot was the neon sign. It featured three naked female silhouettes under the words "LIVE NUDES!" A large man smoking a cigarette and sitting on a wooden stool guarded the entrance. He looked bored.

As we approached, he recited mechanically, "Twenty dollar cover. Each." He didn't mention Skippy. The man looked liked he'd seen everything. Twice.

Nigel reached into his pocket for his wallet. "Okay, but first can I have your assurance that your sign is correct?" he asked jerking his chin toward the marquee.

The man glanced up at the sign. "Yeah," he said. "they're nude."

"That's not the adjective I'm worried about," Nigel said as he handed over the money.

TWENTY-FOUR

INSIDE THE LUCKY LADY, it was loud, dark, and smoky. Music blared from tinny speakers. The walls were mirrored and smudged. Colored lights hung from the black ceiling. Down the middle of the room ran a long wooden catwalk. At its end was a partially naked girl swinging on a pole. Low circular tables crowded with leering men filled the room's remaining space.

A man walked past me on unsteady legs. Seeing me, he gave a low whistle. Seeing Skippy, he came to an abrupt halt. "What the hell is that?" he demanded.

"Part of a new act management wants to try out," said Nigel.

"Jesus," said the man, before wandering away. "This place is awesome."

From across the room, a twitchy little man with a wiry mustache saw us and rushed over. He didn't look happy. "Hey, you can't have a dog in here," he said. "He can't be in here. The Board of Health will shut me down."

"Oh, let's be honest," I said, "If you get shut down, it won't be because of a Board of Health violation. Now who are you?"

"The manager."

"I gathered that. I meant, what's your name? I'll need it for the report."

He took a step back. "Report? What report?"

"The one that is going to cite you for hiring underaged girls," I said, pointing to the glassy-eyed girl gyrating on the stage.

The man glanced behind him. "Hey, she's eighteen. Saw her license and everything. I run a legit business here."

"I'll be sure to mention that in the report. But I still need your name."

He paused. "It's Tim Oberlin."

"Thank you, Mr. Oberlin. Now is there a Leo Blackwell here?"

Tim's eyes widened. "Why? What did he tell you? 'Cause the guy's a drunk. I wouldn't trust anything he said."

"I'll keep that in mind. Where is he?"

Tim jerked his thumb to an area behind him. "He's at a table in the back corner with one of my girls. If you want to talk to him, you'd better do it soon. He's getting pretty loaded."

We walked over to the table Tim indicated. Leo was snuggled up against a busty blonde. Based on her outfit—a corset and fishnet stockings—I guessed that she was between sets. I took a good look at Leo. Thin, with dark hair slicked back, he had high cheekbones and a full mouth. He was the kind of guy whose youth made him good-looking. Once that faded, so, too, would the rest.

I noticed that while his suit was a custom-cut Armani, it was also somewhat the worse for wear. It had the appearance of doing double duty as pajamas.

As we approached, Leo drained his glass and waved to the wait-ress to bring him another. The blonde said, "Honey, slow down. What's the rush? We've got all night."

"No rush," Leo answered, his voice thick. "I'm celebratin'."

Nigel, Skippy, and I stopped at his table. "Well, hello, Leo!" said Nigel brightly, as if he'd just happened upon an old friend. "Fancy meeting you here!"

At the sound of his name, Leo looked up, his gaze unfocused, his expression doubtful. "Do I know you?" he asked.

"Do you know me?" Nigel repeated, as if amused. "Leo, you kill me. How could you forget your wife's favorite cousin?" Pulling up two chairs, he indicated for me to sit in one while he sat in the other. Skippy sat between us and stared at Leo.

"Is that a dog?" asked the blonde.

Nigel pulled his brows together. "What are you talking about?" he asked. "What dog?"

"That dog right there!" she said, pointing at Skippy.

Nigel looked blankly at Skippy and then back at the blonde. "My mother taught me never to contradict a lady." He paused. "You're seeing things."

The blonde narrowed her eyes, unsure of Nigel's meaning. "Lis-ten, baby," she finally said to Leo. "I've got to get ready for my act. Make sure you cheer loud for me, okay?" She stroked her long red nails against his cheek, placed a wet kiss on his mouth, and slid out of her seat. No one said a word to her.

"So, Leo," said Nigel. "How's tricks? Wait, let me rephrase that. How are you? Where've you been?"

"Around. Ya know. Busy." He pronounced this last word as if it was spelled with several "z's." "Did Audrey send you here?" He asked.

"Audrey? No. The little lady and I are here celebrating our anniversary," Nigel said, indicating me. "Leo, this is Nic. I met Nic here three years ago tonight. She was their opening act back then."

I smiled at Leo. "I juggled knives."

"Her stage name was Six-Fingered Sally," Nigel added.

Leo put his glass to his lips and took a long sip. "What d'ya want, Nigel?"

"Well, it's a little embarrassing, but I never got a thank-you card for the wedding gift I sent you. Tell me, did you not like the waffle maker?"

Leo glared at Nigel. "You think you're so damn funny. Well, I'm not laughin'."

"Neither am I, you son of a bitch," countered Nigel, his voice now harsh. "Now, call your wife. For some reason she's worried about you."

Leo shook his head and gave us an odd smile. "She's worried that I won't show up for her party? Well, you can tell her not to be. I'll be home first thing in the morning, and I'll be at her blasted party tomorrow night. Wouldn't miss it for the world. But tonight, I'm celebratin'."

"What are you celebrating?" I asked.

Leo gave a broad grin. "My luck."

The music suddenly switched to The Divinyls "I Touch Myself." The curtains pulled back, and Leo's friend sauntered onto the stage. She waved at Leo and blew him a kiss. I shifted my chair so it faced away from the stage.

"Would this newfound luck of yours have anything to do with what happened to Fat Saul?" I asked Leo.

Leo didn't look at me. His eyes remained fixed on the spectacle behind me. "Yeah. I heard about that. Too bad."

"You owed him money, didn't you?" I asked.

"Yeah. So what? I've got it."

"Is that so? Where'd you get it?" I asked. "From Audrey?"

Leo's mouth curved into a sly smile. "No, not from Audrey. Not directly, anyway. But it seems she is my lucky lady." He started to laugh. "Who'd have ever thought she'd be lucky?"

I reached over and laid a restraining hand on Nigel's fist. "Does Frank know you have his money?" I asked.

Leo watched the stage, still laughing. "Yeah. He knows."

"Really? When I talked to Frank, he said he hadn't heard from you."

"Yeah, well, shows how much you know. As of this morning, we've talked. Ask him yourself, if you don't believe me. I got his money. He knows that. I didn't have a beef with Fat Saul, and I don't have a beef with Frank."

Behind me the crowd gave a hoot of approval. Leo craned his neck to get a better look.

"Seems like Fat Saul might have disagreed with you on that," I said. "I got the impression that he was looking for you the night he died. He might have thought you'd skipped out on him. Tell me, did he find you?"

Leo dragged his eyes away from the stage and glared at me. "What the hell is it to you?"

138

"Nothing," I admitted. "But some friends of mine in the department are kind of curious. I told them I'd ask you if I saw you."

Leo took another sip of his drink. "You a cop?"

I shook my head. "Not anymore. But people around you seem to have a nasty habit of dying."

"You mean like Lizzy?" Leo asked, his eyes suddenly alert.

"Oh, so you know about Lizzy. How did you find out?" I asked.

Leo's eyes shifted away from mine. "Read about it in the papers."

"Papers haven't reported it yet. Besides, I'm not convinced you can actually read. Try again."

"Fine. Frank told me about it when I talked to him," Leo said.

"Really?"

"*Really*. Look, I didn't have anything to do with her death."

"Still," I said, "you have to admit, it might look suspicious to those who aren't cognizant of your stellar reputation."

Leo looked at me, confused. "What did you ... ?" he began, but the crowd began to cheer wildly, and he focused again on the stage. Seconds later, a lacy black bra flew through the air and landed on our table. Leo went to grab it, but Skippy got to it first. He sat back, the bra dangling partially out of his mouth, and resumed staring at Leo.

I sighed. Leo was drunk and belligerent. I wasn't going to get anything more out of him tonight. Nothing coherent, anyway. "Okay," I said, pushing my chair back and standing up. "I don't have anything more to say. Nigel, did you want to say anything?"

Without a sound, Nigel stood up and slugged Leo across the jaw. Leo toppled off his chair and landed in a messy heap on the floor.

"No, I'm good," he said. Shaking out his hand a few times, he offered me his arm.

"May I see you home, Mrs. Martini?" he asked.

"I'd be delighted, Mr. Martini," I answered.

TWENTY-FIVE

THE NEXT MORNING WE were awakened once again by the sound of the phone. Nigel briefly looked at it before burying his head back into his pillow. "Remind me to have that damned thing disconnected," he said. "It's an utter nuisance."

The phone continued to ring. I poked him. "It's an utter nuisance which is A: On your side of the bed and B: Most likely from one of *your* relatives."

"You don't know that," Nigel mumbled. "It could be from one of yours."

"Doubtful. My family has the good sense not to call before ten a.m."

"You forget your Aunt Martha."

"That's true. But as she's been dead for over a year now, I don't think it's her."

"You may have a point there," he said, grabbing for the receiver. "But we'll see who has the last laugh if you're wrong."

"If I'm wrong, I don't think anyone will be laughing."

"Hello?" Nigel said, his voice hopeful. "Aunt Martha?" He paused. "Oh, hello, Aunt Olive."

I smiled, wiggled my fingers at him, and snuggled back under the covers. "No, I wasn't asleep," I heard him say. "Of course not. Why would I be at … seven-twenty in the morning? No, actually, Nic and I were just concluding a most utopian-like … hmmm? No, I suppose you wouldn't want to hear about it. I see. Really. I see. Well, that is interesting. What? No, we can't come over for breakfast. No, I'm sorry. I know. I know. Okay. Okay. Okay. That's right. Bye."

"So, what time do we have to be there for breakfast?" I asked from under the covers.

"Nine-thirty."

I sighed. "I think I would have preferred Aunt Martha after all."

———

As requested, we arrived at Aunt Olive's at nine-thirty. "Well, Leo's back," Olive said, in lieu of a greeting when we entered the room. She was sitting in her favorite chair, wearing a gold silk pantsuit and a peevish expression. Her fingers drummed an angry tom-tom on the armrest. "He showed up early this morning on Audrey's doorstep, flowers in hand, to beg for forgiveness," she bit out. She then remarked at length on both Leo's canine heritage and his mother's marital status, before ending with a dire prognostication as to the fate of his soul.

Across from her on the couch, Daphne sipped coffee from a delicate teacup. She also appeared to be in a less-than-joyous mood. Her face seemed thinner, and her eyes were dull. She gave us a half wave and then returned to her coffee.

"Where's Max?" Nigel asked.

"On the phone. *Again,*" groused Olive. "I swear to God he spends more time on that damn thing than with me." Max poked his head out from the kitchen doorway. There were dark circles under his eyes. He held a phone to his ear with one hand. With the other he indicated that he'd be out in a minute. He quickly ducked back into the kitchen.

Olive glared at the space where his head had just been. "See what I mean?" she said.

"Mother, I'm sure it's just business," said Daphne, her voice tired.

"Well, of course, it's just business," Olive snapped. "What else would it be?"

No one answered. Moments later, Max reappeared, the phone gone. "Good morning, Nic. Good morning, Nigel," he said, his voice tired. "Can I get you some coffee?"

"Yes, please," we answered.

He disappeared back into the kitchen. Nigel and I sat down. "What does Audrey say about all of this?" I asked.

Olive rolled her eyes. "I don't really know. I don't think Audrey does either. She was clearly relieved not to have to face the party tonight alone, but she is also angry, hurt, and confused."

"That's understandable," I said. "What does she plan to do about Leo's debt? Is she going to pay it off?"

"I don't know that either. I didn't think to ask her. She just called us early this morning to tell us the 'good' news that the jackass was back and would be in attendance tonight. It wasn't a very long conversation." She glared at us.

"I don't understand, Aunt Olive," Nigel said. "I was under the impression that you *wanted* Leo to come home in time for Audrey's party. Well, the party is tonight. You got your wish. I thought you'd be happy."

The tom-tom beat abruptly stopped. "Happy? *Happy*? Are you insane? Haven't you seen this morning's paper?"

"No, actually, I haven't," Nigel said.

Olive reached down to the floor beside her. Picking up a newspaper, she slammed it down on the coffee table in front of us. "Now what do you say?"

I looked down. It was the *Post*. In large print, the headline read: "The Martini Knockout." Underneath was a picture taken of us last night. It was a spectacular shot of Nigel's fist connecting with Leo's jaw. It was a little blurry, but there was no doubt that it was us. I was standing next to Nigel, a surprised expression on my face. Next to me was Skippy, the black bra hanging out of his mouth.

"Oh," Nigel said.

"Oh?" repeated Olive. "Is that all you can say? *Oh*?"

"Well, there's no sale at Penney's, so I guess 'Oh,' will have to do."

"It's outrageous! First of all, why didn't you tell me that you had located him?" Olive fumed. "And second of all, why were you in a strip joint?"

"We got a tip that Leo was there, so we went there. As you can see, the tip was right." Pointing at the picture, I said, "What you see here is merely Nigel convincing Leo that he needed to go home." I paused and then added, "Apparently, it worked because he did just that."

Nigel smiled at Olive. "You're welcome."

"Have you no sense?" Olive snapped. "This kind of press is a nightmare. And on the day of the party, too!"

Daphne regarded her mother with irritation. "Calm down, Mother. Why don't you take one of your pills?"

Max came back into the room with the coffee tray. Putting it down squarely on top of the paper, he said, "Olive, dear, it is what it is. There's no use yelling at anyone, least of all Nic and Nigel."

Olive crossed her arms and took a deep breath. Finally, she tipped her head in agreement. "I suppose you're right," she said grudgingly. "Besides, we have more important issues to deal with."

Max handed me a cup of coffee. "What issues?" I asked.

Max did not answer. He handed Nigel a cup.

"Audrey's birthday is tomorrow," Olive said. "Which means that we have exactly one day to convince her not to pay off Leo's debt."

Daphne sighed. "I think that ship has sailed, Mother."

Olive shot her an annoyed look. "Nonsense. I am quite confident that if we all put our heads together, we can think of *something*."

Max poured himself a cup and sat down. "Well, short of killing the SOB I don't see what we can do."

Olive sighed. "Daphne, be a dear and fetch me my pills. I feel another attack coming on."

TWENTY-SIX

IT STARTED SNOWING EARLY that afternoon. By nightfall, the city was covered with a shimmery white powder that made driving a nightmare. However, despite the inclement weather, Audrey's guests, who no doubt had also seen the *Post*, were not going to miss this event. When Nigel and I made our way downstairs to the Olmsted ballroom, the party was in full swing and full attendance. A white-tuxedoed band was serenading a crowded dance floor. Waiters assigned with the Sisyphean task of serving champagne busily circled the room carrying silver trays loaded with crystal flutes. Men were laughing. Women were gossiping. Small children were at home with their nannies as Olive—in the spirit of the holidays— had deemed them *persona non grata*. Select members of various publications were in attendance as well. Olive had insisted that "the elite press" cover the event. I didn't comment on that decision. It was her oxymoron, not mine.

On the back wall, above a multi-tiered birthday cake, a projector flashed enormous images of Audrey culled from over the years—from her lolling about in a diaper to her lolling about on a yacht. Nigel and I paused in the doorway and took in the raucous scene before us. "Well, this was fun, don't you think, Mrs. Martini?" Nigel said to me.

"Oodles, Mr. Martini," I agreed.

"But I think—sadly—that it's time to leave."

"I quite agree. We don't want to overstay our welcome," I said.

"I'll get our coats."

"We're not wearing any," I pointed out. "We came from upstairs."

"Excellent. One less step to worry about."

We each took a cautious step backward when a voice called out our names. "Nigel! Nicole!"

I turned to see Olive, resplendent in a red satin ball gown, bearing down on us, her expression dire.

"Dear God," said Nigel. "As I live and breath, it's the Red Queen."

I pasted a polite smile on my face and prepared for the worst. Her displeasure, however, was not aimed at me. "Absolutely not! No. I forbid it. Nigel Martini, you are not bringing that dog into this party!" she said.

Nigel glanced down at Skippy. "Why ever not?" he asked.

"You know exactly why not," Olive fumed.

Nigel affected a look of understanding. "Oh, right. The invitation. Black tie only. But never fear, Auntie dear, Skippy is dressed appropriately." He lifted up Skippy's massive head to reveal the black on black silk paisley tie that was neatly knotted around his neck. "I think he looks rather dapper, actually," Nigel added in a confidential whisper. Skippy barked and wagged his tail.

"Nigel..." Olive said through clenched teeth.

I raised my hand. "I completely understand, Olive," I said. "Perhaps this isn't an appropriate place for Skippy. We'll be happy to take him back to our room."

Olive's mouth turned up in a relieved smile. "Thank you, Nicole. I just don't think... wait," she paused, giving me a searching look. "You are coming back though, right?"

"I don't think so," said Nigel. "It'll be impossible to get a sitter at this late date, especially as most of the eligible ones are already busy tonight. But don't worry. We'll just say a quick hello and good-bye to Audrey and then be on our way."

Olive grabbed Nigel's arm as he moved to turn away. "You'll do no such thing." With a reluctant sigh, she said, "Fine. He can stay. But please try to keep an eye on him. He can be a bit... startling."

"You won't even notice he's here," Nigel promised.

Olive raised her eyebrow. "Yes, well. As long as I notice that *you're* here, that's fine. Now go say hello to Audrey. She's over there," Olive said, indicating a large table in the center of the room.

We dutifully made our way over to where Audrey stood with Leo talking to a few guests. She was wearing a long silver gown with a deep, narrow neckline. Her hair was slicked back. Her makeup was more elaborate than usual, but it still didn't hide the fact that she was pale and there were faint blue circles under her eyes. Leo stood next to her giving every appearance of the devoted husband. He wore the required black tux, which normally elevates any man's appearance. On Leo it just looked like he sold a better brand of used cars. I noticed that he was sporting a new bruise on his face thanks to Nigel's parting shot last night. As we approached, Audrey and Leo saw us and smiled. Only one was genuine.

"Nic! Nigel!" Audrey said, after excusing herself from her other guests. "I'm so glad you could be here." Turning back to Leo, she said, "Leo, I don't think you've ever met my cousin Nigel's wife. Nic, this is Leo. Leo, meet Nic."

Around us, all the guests surreptitiously watched Leo and Nigel while pretending to do otherwise. Leo rolled his eyes. "We've met, Audrey. The whole room knows that we've met. There is a lovely photo on the front page of today's *Post* documenting that meeting. So, let's not pretend otherwise, shall we?"

"Please, Leo," Audrey pleaded through a fake smile. "Everyone is watching."

Leo, obliging, pasted on his own fake smile. "Fine. It was great to see you last night, Nigel. I look forward to suing you for assault. An assault that was happily captured on camera."

Nigel smiled as well. "Nothing gave me greater pleasure! In fact, I look forward to doing it again. And the only thing a jury would convict me of would be not hitting you harder."

Audrey winced, but said nothing. "That's enough," I said. "You're making Audrey uncomfortable. Happy birthday, Audrey. You look lovely, by the way."

"As do you, Leo," added Nigel. "By the way, how do you get your tux so shiny?"

Audrey pretended not to hear Nigel. To me she said, "Thank you, Nic. I love your dress. You should wear pink more often."

"Why, thank you," I said. "But you know, the zipper isn't latching right. Would you please be a dear and help me with it? I asked Nigel, but he's all thumbs."

"Um ... sure, of course," Audrey stammered, taking a tentative step toward me.

"Oh, thanks," I said. "Not here, though. Where are the restrooms?"

"Over there ..." Audrey began.

Leo interrupted her. "I don't think you should leave your guests, Audrey," he said. "I'm sure someone else can help Nic with her problem."

"Oh, but we'll only be a minute," I said as I pulled Audrey away. Nigel quickly stepped between Leo and us and said, "Do you mind watching Skippy for me for a minute, Leo? I'm going to get a drink. Just be careful what you say around him. He's been trained to attack when he hears a common everyday phrase."

Leo's eyes grew wide, and he stared cautiously at Skippy. "What is it?" he asked.

"No, but you're close," said Nigel. "I'll be right back."

I dragged Audrey across the room and out of the ballroom. Finding a quiet corner, I turned to her. "What is going on? Why are you behaving like a scared rabbit?"

Audrey stared back at me, her brown eyes deceptively wide. "Nothing's going on. Leo came home and told me everything. He's very sorry. He said he just needed to blow off a little steam."

"Blow off a little steam? He disappeared for several days!"

"I know," Audrey said quickly, her cheeks flushing a dark red. "But he's sorry. I'm sure he'll never do it again."

"You don't really believe that, do you?" I asked.

Audrey nodded her head. "I do. I told him that I knew he owed people money and that I would take care of it only if he promised to go to Gamblers Anonymous."

"And he agreed?"

She nodded. "He had to. How else is he going to pay it?"

I didn't say anything. Leo certainly had had money last night and made it sound as if he'd already paid Frank back. If that were true, then he hadn't gotten it from Audrey. So, who had he gotten it from?

I changed the subject. "What about Lizzy Marks? Did you tell him that you knew about the two of them?"

She looked down, suddenly fascinated with the carpet. "He ... he told me about her. They ... were just friends. They were more than that once, but it's over now."

"Well, it would have to be, Audrey. The poor woman's dead."

Audrey flinched as if I slapped her. "I'm sorry, Audrey. I don't mean to tell you your business." I paused. "No, that's not true. I don't *want* to tell you your business, but clearly someone needs to shove some sense into your head. Leo is a slime bag who is only interested in your money. He is using you. Tomorrow you will turn twenty-five and will gain control over your trust. There will be no Aunt Olive and Uncle Leo to protect you from yourself. It seems to me that if you're old enough to be deemed responsible to manage that size fortune then you should be responsible period."

Audrey's face bunched, and her eyes welled with tears. As a rule, I don't kick puppies. However, watching Audrey now, I felt that I had an inkling as to what it must feel like.

Audrey slowly raised her head. "Please don't hate me," she said in a small voice, "but ..."

"Audrey! There you are! Whatever are you doing out here? You have guests to attend to!" I turned to see Olive marching across the lobby, her red dress trailing out behind her, her expression grim.

Audrey gave me an agonized look and then turned away. "I was just helping Nic with her zipper," she called out in a practiced cheerful voice.

Olive shot me a doubtful glance. "Well, this is more important than a zipper," she said, extending her hand to Audrey. "Mrs. Otterson is asking for you."

I remained standing where I was. It was clear that Mrs. Otterson's interest did not extend to me. Which was fine. I wanted to think.

TWENTY-SEVEN

AFTER ABOUT TWENTY MINUTES, Nigel came out into the lobby carrying two glasses of champagne. "Here you are," he said as he crossed to where I was sitting. Taking a seat next to me on the leather settee, he said, "I was wondering where you went." There was a smudge of red lipstick on his right cheek. I reached over and rubbed it off with my thumb.

"I don't think this is your shade, by the way," I said as I took one of the glasses. I took a sip and asked, "Where's Skippy?"

"With the owner of the lipstick, a delightful woman named Rose. Apparently, she once had a Vaudeville act that included a dog and a monkey. She's trying to teach Skippy the basics."

"Which part? The dog's or the monkey's?"

"Does it really matter?" he asked.

"Probably not," I admitted.

"How's Audrey?" Nigel asked.

"Well, that's an interesting question. She seems nervous. And unstable. And about ten other anxiety-induced traits. Why don't we just go with 'A Hot Mess' and leave it at that."

"A hot mess who is about to inherit an enormous fortune," Nigel corrected.

"Right. A hot mess who is about to inherit an enormous fortune and who is married to a gold-digging louse."

Nigel leaned back. "I really wish this weekend was over," he said.

I clinked my glass against his. "Me too."

As we came back into the ballroom, we bumped into Nigel's parents. Paul was handsome in a fitted tux. Doris looked lovely as always. She was wearing a strapless gown of midnight blue that fell in graceful folds to the floor. Her face was bright with laughter. "Can I just tell you how much I love your dog?" she said.

Paul wrapped his arm around Doris's waist and grinned at us. "Your mother is quite enamored with Skippy. She was rewarding him with the bacon and scallop hors d'oeuvres."

Doris nodded. "He seemed to prefer those over the crab puffs."

"Well, don't we all?" mused Nigel.

"Can he visit us sometime?" Doris asked. "I'd love to introduce him to Chloe."

"The alpaca?" I asked.

Doris nodded. "She's very gentle, and she needs a friend closer to her own size. Our poodle, Muffin, scares the crap out of her."

"Muffin scares the crap out of everyone, Mother. Including me," said Nigel.

"Speaking of crap, I guess you saw that Leo is back," said a thick voice behind my shoulder. I turned to see Toby. His eyes were glassy and, despite the excellent fit of his custom-made tux, he appeared disheveled. "I really hoped he was gone for good this time," he said, glaring to where Leo sat alone at his table.

"So did everyone," said Nigel.

Toby shook his head. "He's a rat son-of-a-bitch. Why couldn't he have just stayed gone? He only makes her miserable."

Daphne appeared at my side. She was wearing a deep sapphire gown that hugged and dipped in all the right places. Her hair was arranged in one of those casual upsweeps that are anything but. "What are we talking about?" she asked.

"The doomed love affair of our very own Romeo and Juliet," Nigel answered. "Audrey and Leo."

Daphne rolled her eyes. "I wouldn't compare them to Romeo and Juliet. For one thing, you were sad when they died. No one would shed a tear if Leo dropped dead."

"Why is it that everyone can see what a louse he is, except for Audrey?" Toby asked.

"I don't know," said Nigel. We all turned to stare at Leo. "Unfortunately, Audrey seems to be the only one who hasn't been able to grasp that point yet."

"Someday she will, but by then it'll be too late," Toby said.

"Unfortunately, I think you are correct," said Nigel. "But there's not much we can do about it."

"There has to be *something*," Toby protested.

"And yet, there is not," said Nigel.

"Are you here alone, Toby?" I asked, hoping to appear as if I were merely changing the subject when in fact I was being nosey.

Toby looked at me blankly. "Am I what?"

"Did you bring a date?" I asked.

Daphne turned on him. "That's right!" she exclaimed. "Since when did you start dating Susan Henkley? Are you out of your mind? She's poison!"

"What? I ... how ... who said I was dating her?" Toby stammered.

"You practically had your tongue down her throat the other night at Baxter's!" Daphne said.

Toby seemed to lose control of this muscle now and regarded Daphne wide-eyed. "Well, that certainly is an image I didn't want shoved into my head," said Nigel.

"Is she here?" Daphne continued.

"I don't think so," Toby answered finally. "At least I didn't bring her."

"Are you dating her?" Daphne pressed.

"What? No. No!" said Toby, his voice agitated.

"Well, then you really should keep your tongue out of her throat," advised Nigel. "That's what's known as serving the hors d'oeuvre no one ordered."

Olive suddenly joined our group. "What are you talking about?" she asked.

"Hors d'oeuvres," Nigel answered.

Olive smiled. "They are good, aren't they? The caterer I hired is the best in the city."

Nigel nodded. "That's what Toby was just saying."

Two women now came up to our group. They appeared to be in their early sixties. One was tall and fleshy, with large brown eyes and a full mouth. Her hair was blonde but her eyebrows were black. She wore an elaborately detailed velvet gown that was a shade somewhere between olive and avocado. Around her neck was a choker of sparkling emeralds. Stones of the same style and cut hung from her plump earlobes. The second woman was built on a smaller scale. From her mouth to her frame, she was all sharp edges and hard lines. Her ensemble was a simple dress of black silk. The only jewelry she wore was a gold wedding band on her left hand. Her gray hair was styled into a short, faintly androgynous bob.

Seeing them, Olive adopted the wide smile she reserved for those acquaintances she didn't actually like. It was one I was very familiar with.

"Marcia! Janet!" Olive cried as she leaned in to give each their allotted air-kiss. "How are you, darlings? You both look lovely! It's so good to see you! Are you having a nice time?"

The larger of the two women spoke first. "Everything is just perfect, Olive. I don't know how you managed all this—and over Christmas as well!"

"Yes," said the smaller woman, "Marcia and I were just saying what an amazing party this is. And Audrey looks so lovely! She and that husband of hers certainly make quite the couple! He's a handsome devil. I bet he keeps her on her toes."

Olive's smile dimmed slightly. "Yes, well, I'm glad you are enjoying yourselves. Marcia, Janet, I don't think you've met Nigel's wife." Turning to me, she continued. "This is Nicole."

I smiled and said a polite hello while Marcia (the flamboyant one) and Janet (the conservative one) eyed me with interest. "It's nice to finally meet you, Nicole," said Marcia.

"Please, call me Nic," I said.

"Yes," said Nigel. "Nicole's just her stage name. We thought it gave the act some class."

Marcia and Janet's eyes opened very wide. "Nigel's just kidding, of course," Olive hissed through a smile.

"I am?" Nigel responded, his forehead crinkled in confusion.

"Nigel!" Olive barked.

Nigel smiled and turned to Janet. "So, Mrs. Harris. I understand my aunt has you to thank for her new butler."

A sly look crept into Janet's gray eyes. "Oh, is he working out?" she asked Olive. "I'm so glad. Joe certainly is a find." Next to her, Marcia began to busy herself with something in her purse.

"*Joseph* has been very helpful," Olive said. "I'm very much in your debt, Janet. You were a darling to suggest him for me."

"Don't be silly, Olive dear," Janet replied with a smile. "It was the *least* I could do. But speaking of staff, dear, I do think you might need to speak with your head of catering."

Olive sensed an attack. She stiffened her spine. "Yes?"

"Well, I just thought you should know that one of your waiters was very rude to us," Janet continued. Her tone held just the right amount of sympathetic distress.

"Is that so?" Olive said. "How?"

"Well," Janet paused as if embarrassed to have to relay such unfortunate information. "Marcia and I tried to order a drink from him, and he quite ignored us! I know that he heard me too. He looked right at us, but he walked away without saying a word."

Olive adopted a stoic expression. "Thank you for letting me know. I will certainly look into it. Do you remember what he looked like?"

Janet wrinkled her beak of a nose and nodded. "Not very attractive, I must say. Big. Short dark hair. And he had a tattoo! Now you know, I'm not one to judge, especially on appearances. But I do think those things ought to be covered up when one is working. It's unseemly." She smiled sweetly at Olive. "Don't you agree, dear?"

"Yes, of course. I'll look into it immediately. I'm sorry for the inconvenience."

"Oh, please, don't worry a thing about it. *We're* fine. I just thought *you'd* want to know. Now. Where is that handsome husband of yours? He promised me a dance." Spying Max a few feet away, Janet added with an innocent air, "And, of course, I need to speak with him about the upcoming charity ball." Turning to me, she added, "It was lovely to meet you, Nicole."

"Likewise," I said.

The two women moved toward Max, but not before I heard them start to giggle. I turned to Olive and, with as much sincerity as I could, said, "They seem nice."

TWENTY-EIGHT

NIGEL AND I WERE sitting quietly at a table when it happened. Olive had just cut in on Janet and Max after their third dance. She and Max were twirling and spinning to the band's music when a high-pitched wailing sound made itself heard. I looked over at Nigel in confusion, unsure if I was interpreting the sound correctly. From the alarmed expression on his face, I knew that I was. The rest of the crowd suddenly became aware of it as well. The dancers slowed and then stopped. People glanced around uneasily. Finally, someone caught the attention of the band leader, and the music came to an abrupt halt. The awful silence that followed was cut by a woman's hysterical screams.

Bedlam ensued as people tried to locate the source. It was found standing at the ballroom's entrance. It was Audrey. Her silver dress was smeared with blood. In her hand was a knife. It, too, was covered in blood. "He's dead!" she screamed. "Dead! Leo! Someone's killed Leo!"

Amidst several camera flashes from the press, Audrey collapsed to the floor. More cameras flashed.

After an initial hush of shock, the guests began screaming and crowding their way out of the ballroom. The bandleader grabbed the microphone and pleaded for everyone to remain calm. I appreciated his quick thinking, but I did wonder what kind of venues he normally played for him to react so calmly. Nigel and I pushed our way through the panicked crowd to where Audrey lay on the ground sobbing.

I grabbed a napkin off a nearby table. Using it, I reached over and gently took the knife out of her shaking hand. Nigel wrapped his arm around her shoulders, picked her up, and steered her to a nearby chair. "Where is he?" I asked. "Where is Leo?"

Audrey covered her face with her hands. Then, realizing they were covered in blood, pulled them away. "He's in there," she said, pointing toward the entrance of the men's room.

Leaving Nigel to calm her down, I went to where Audrey had indicated. Just inside the door was a lounge area with several club chairs. Leo was sprawled on the floor in front of one. His eyes stared unseeingly at the ceiling. I slowly walked to him. He was covered in blood. It appeared that he'd been stabbed in the back. From the position of his body, it seemed likely that he'd been seated when he'd been stabbed. I bent down and felt for the pulse that I knew wasn't there. Then I opened my purse and took out my phone.

"Marcy? Hi, it's me. Listen, I might need your help tonight. Someone's killed Leo Blackwell."

"Seriously?" she said. Her voice was sleepy. I glanced at my watch. It was a little after midnight. "Where are you?"

"In the men's room of the Ritz. Leo's here on the floor."

Marcy swore. "Did you find him?"

"No. Audrey did."

"Well, don't touch anything. Has someone called it in?"

"I think so," I replied, trying not to look at Leo's face anymore.

"Okay. Well, I'll call it just in case. Do you want me to come?"

"If it's not too much trouble," I answered.

"Okay. I'll be there as soon as I can. You know the drill, though. Don't touch anything, and don't move the body."

"Yeah, about that first part ..."

"What?"

"Audrey was the one who found him. She picked up the knife."

Marcy swore again. "That's not good, Nic."

"I know," I sighed. "That's why I called you."

———

I hung up with Marcy and went out to the lobby. The hotel staff was on the phone with the police and their own higher-ups. I told a woman behind the front desk to assign someone from hotel security to guard the entrance to the bathroom. She nodded at everything I said, her face pale with horror. "So, it's true, then? Someone died in the bathroom?" she asked, her voice a high squeak.

"The guest of honor's husband," I answered. "Did you see anything?"

The woman shook her head. "No. I just heard the screaming. When I looked up, I saw that woman standing in the doorway covered in blood."

I thanked her and walked back to where Nigel sat with Audrey. He was trying to get her to drink something. Olive and Max crowded around her as well. "Audrey," I said, "tell me everything that happened."

I pulled up a chair next to hers and waited.

"I ... didn't know where Leo was," she began. "I couldn't find him. Aunt Olive said that it was almost time to cut the cake and that Leo needed to be with me." Her voice broke. Nigel squeezed her hand. "I couldn't find him," she repeated.

"Why did you go into the men's room?" I asked.

Audrey looked at me, her eyes dazed. "It was the only place I hadn't looked. I thought maybe he was ... in there."

I stared back at her. "You didn't think to ask one of the male guests to check for you?"

Audrey shook her head. "No. I thought ..." she looked down at her hands. Seeing the blood on them, she quickly jerked her gaze away. "I wondered if he ... I just wanted to see ..."

"You wanted to see if he was fooling around with someone in the bathroom?" I finished for her.

She averted her eyes from mine. "Yes," she whispered. Seeing my look of disbelief, she added, "It's happened before."

"Oh, Audrey, my poor darling!" Olive said, as she stroked Audrey's hair. Looking around, she asked, "You had a knife. Where did it go?"

Audrey looked down. "I don't know," she glanced vaguely around for the item in question.

"I have it," I said.

Audrey closed her eyes. "I picked up the knife," she said dully. "The one used to kill Leo."

"Do you mean someone stabbed him?" Olive screeched.

I looked at her in annoyance. "That would seem to be the case."

"But why would anyone do that?" Olive asked. "This is the Ritz for God's sake!"

"Yes, well, I'll speak to management about that when I get a moment," I said. Focusing again on Audrey, I continued, "Audrey? Do you feel okay? Can I get you anything?"

Audrey shook her head. "No, I'm okay. But ... but what am I going to do?"

"Don't worry about a thing," said Max. "We'll take care of it."

Daphne and Toby rushed up. Daphne gave Audrey an awkward hug, trying not to get any of Leo's blood on her own dress. "Audrey! Oh my God, you poor thing. How did it happen?" Without waiting for an answer, she continued, "This is a nightmare!"

Toby pulled up a chair next to Audrey's. He handed her a wet napkin to clean her hands. She smiled gratefully at him and began to rub at the blood. "Have you called the police?" she asked.

I nodded. "The hotel staff called. I also talked to one of my former colleagues. She's on her way as well."

Olive looked at me sharply. "Why on earth would you do that?" she asked.

"I have a feeling that Audrey is going to need all the help she can get," I said, my tone matter-of-fact.

"What the hell is that supposed to mean?" she snapped at me. "How dare you infer ..."

"Imply," corrected Nigel.

"... that Audrey had anything to do with that man's death! Why, I'm sure there are loads of people who wanted Leo dead!" Olive glared at me and then belatedly realized her blunder. Turning back to Audrey, she said, "Oh, Audrey. I'm sorry. I didn't mean it like that. I just want to protect you." Olive's eyes welled with tears, and she blindly grabbed Max's hand for comfort.

Audrey didn't respond. I did. "Olive, I'm not saying that Audrey killed Leo. However, she did go into the men's room and because she picked up the knife that killed him, her fingerprints will be all over that knife. Thanks to yesterday's article and accompanying photograph, half of New York knows that their marriage was in trouble. Those facts alone are going to guarantee a police investigation into Audrey's possible motives for killing Leo. And God help her if it comes out that she went to Lizzy Marks's apartment and not only found her dead, but then said nothing about her discovery to the authorities."

"What are you saying?" Audrey asked, her voice dull.

"Among other things, you need to tell the police about your visit to Lizzy Marks's house," I said.

Toby disagreed. Rather strongly. "Absolutely not!" he hissed, quickly looking around to make sure no one could hear us. "I told you before what I thought of that idea. They'll crucify her!"

"What do you think they'll do once they figure out that she was there and never came forward?" I asked.

"There is no law that says she has to do anything. She is under no obligation to go to the police to report the death of a person that is already known to be dead. You of all people should know that. As her lawyer, I will make sure she understands that," Toby said.

"Well, for a lawyer, I think you're giving her pretty crappy advice. The press is going to go crazy with this."

Toby sighed. "Look, Nic, I get what you're saying, but I don't think this is the time or the place to discuss this. She just found her husband dead—murdered. I think it would be extremely foolish to say anything now. Not until we have a game plan."

I looked at Audrey. She was staring at the floor, a dazed expression on her face. I realized that as much as I disagreed with Toby in principle, he probably did have a point. To make Audrey tell the police about her visit to Lizzy Marks now would probably result in her immediate arrest.

TWENTY-NINE

MARCY ARRIVED SOON AFTER the other police. She found me and I told her what I knew. Which, admittedly, wasn't much.

"So, Audrey says she couldn't find Leo and went to look for him?" Marcy asked me.

"Yes. I guess they were about to cut her birthday cake."

"And she went looking for him in the men's room why?"

I shrugged. "I think she was suspicious that he might have been entertaining a guest there."

Marcy raised an eyebrow. "In the men's bathroom?"

"Well, in the men's bathroom at the Ritz. You have to admit, it's a cut above your average bathroom. But, to answer your question, yes. She thought he might be in there with someone. Apparently, he'd done it before."

Marcy shook her head in disgust. "Real classy guy, this Leo was."

"That he was," I agreed.

"So, she finds him on the floor, covered in blood. She grabs the knife—why?"

"I have no idea. I think she was in shock. She ran out of the bathroom and into the ballroom and started screaming. I went into the bathroom and saw Leo on the floor. I made sure the hotel posted security at the bathroom's entrance and called you. What do you think they're going to do to Audrey?" I asked.

Marcy looked over to where Audrey sat talking with the lead detective, Tom Cutter. Marcy didn't look optimistic. "I don't know, Nic," she said. "Cutter's a nice guy, but he's also pretty cynical. I don't know if he's going to buy her story about trying to catch Leo in the act."

I looked at her. "Do you buy it?"

Marcy didn't answer right away. "I don't know, Nic. I wish I could tell you different, but I just don't know. But it's not up to me. It depends on whether Tom Cutter believes her."

———

As it turned out, Tom Cutter did believe Audrey, but he made it clear that it was not a binding decision. Olive was, to say the least, outraged that Audrey could in any way be considered a suspect, and to prove her point screamed at the police. When they finally left, she turned her fury on me. It was only after Nigel and I returned to our rooms and took the phone off the hook that the yelling stopped.

THIRTY

THE PAPERS HAD A field day with Leo's murder and Audrey's discovery of the body. They all stopped short of setting themselves up for being sued for libel, but only by a hair. There were two schools of thought. One was that Audrey killed Leo in a drunken fit fueled by jealously. The second was that she deliberately killed him to rid herself of a two-timing cash hound. The only difference between the two theories, really, was a few drinks.

Nigel and I sat in our hotel room reading the various versions of the story. "This one says Leo was stabbed in the chest," said Nigel. "And this one," he pointed to a different paper, "says he was stabbed in the neck."

"Well, he wasn't," I said. "Not that it matters in the end. He was stabbed, and he's dead, and everyone thinks Audrey did it. Why the hell did she pick up the knife? Who does that?"

"Audrey, apparently," said Nigel.

"This isn't good, Nigel," I said. "In fact, this is really bad."

"Yes, dear. I know. I might be new to all this, but I did gather that much. The question is, what are we going to about it?"

A knock on our hotel door saved me from having to answer this. It was Daphne.

"I'm sorry to bother you like this, Nic," she said.

"Not at all," I said. "Come on in. Nigel and I were just reading the paper. How's Audrey?"

Daphne followed me into the front room where Nigel was sprawled on the couch. "She's finally sleeping, thank God. We gave her a sedative from Mother's private stash." She took off her coat and laid it over the back of the desk chair. For once, she seemed a loss for words.

"Can I get you a drink?" Nigel asked.

"Yes, please. Do you have any vodka?"

"I think so," I answered.

"Fine," said Daphne. "Mix it with anything you've got, or I'll take it straight."

I glanced at Nigel. As it was only 9:30 in the morning, I had been thinking more along the lines of coffee. Nigel shrugged.

While I made her a drink, Nigel said, "What's wrong, Daphne?"

"Besides the fact that someone killed Leo and the police suspect Audrey?" she asked.

"Is there a besides?"

Daphne looked down. I finished making her drink and handed it to her. She took a long sip. "Yes," she finally said. "There is a 'besides.' This is really awkward, but I need to ask Nic something about Leo."

I sat down next to Nigel. "Fire away."

Daphne took another sip. "When you found him, was there … was there any money on him?"

"Money?" I repeated. "I don't know. I checked his pulse, not his wallet. Why?"

Daphne's cheeks flushed red. "It's just that … this is awkward, but I'd given Leo money earlier that night. A great deal of it actually."

"Why?" I asked.

Daphne glanced down before answering. "Blackmail. Leo saw Audrey leaving that woman's apartment. Lizzy. You know, the one who was killed?"

"I'm familiar with the situation, Daphne," I said.

"Right. Of course you are. Sorry. Anyway, Leo saw Audrey coming out of Lizzy's apartment. Audrey didn't see him. He went in after she left and found Lizzy dead. Leo told me that unless I paid him off, he was going to go to the police and tell them that Audrey killed Lizzy. I told him he was crazy and that no one would believe him, but then he said that if I paid him, he'd leave. Forever."

"Why did he come to you?" I asked. "I would have thought he would have gone to Max or your mother."

Daphne raised an eyebrow. "Are you kidding? Can you imagine the scene my mother would create if Leo tried to blackmail *her*? Leo had gumption, but not *that* much gumption."

"Point taken. When did this happen?" I asked.

"He called me the morning of Audrey's party," Daphne said. "He said that I was to give him the money at the party or he'd go to the police. He promised to stay for the party, and then he would leave Audrey for good."

"Just like that?" I asked.

"Well, not exactly. He wanted me to deposit money into an account for him every month. The amount wasn't outrageous. We could afford it."

"Who's we?" I asked.

"The family," Daphne said, flushing a little. "I was going to talk to my dad about it and see what we could do."

"Did Audrey know about this?" Nigel asked.

"Of course not! I couldn't tell her. But I agreed to it. I didn't want Audrey hauled up on charges of murdering that woman! Audrey didn't kill her. I know that, but the police might not see it the same way. And here was a chance to get Leo out of her life. For good!"

"Seems that happened anyway," said Nigel.

"Well, yes," agreed Daphne. "But I didn't know that was going to happen. I just wanted to protect Audrey."

I tried to piece together what Daphne was saying. "How much money did you give him?" I asked.

When she told me the amount, I stood up and made myself a drink with vodka as well. "Better make me one, too, darling," said Nigel.

When I returned to the couch, I handed Nigel his drink. "Where did you get that kind of money, Daphne?" I asked, hoping I was wrong about the answer I suspected I was going to hear.

Daphne flushed red. "Audrey's trust fund. I took it out of the trust."

THIRTY-ONE

I EXCUSED MYSELF AND left Nigel to deal with Daphne. From the bedroom I called Marcy. "Money?" she repeated after I asked her my question. "No, there wasn't any money found on the body. Why?"

I repeated what Daphne had told me. Well, minus the part where Leo was blackmailing Daphne about Audrey's presence at Lizzy's. I just left it that Daphne was paying Leo to leave. Marcy let out a low whistle. "Lord, Nic. That complicates things a bit."

"It might. But then again, it might help Audrey's case. If Leo was killed for the money, then it lets Audrey off the hook."

"How so?"

"Audrey didn't have to kill Leo in the men's room if she wanted the money. She could have just taken it out of his pocket when they got home."

"Or she might have found out about his plan to leave her and killed him out of anger. God knows, I'd be tempted if I were her. Who besides Daphne knew about the money?"

"I don't know if anyone knew."

"Well, clearly *someone* knew," said Marcy. "Because it's gone now."

———

When I returned to the living room, I told Daphne and Nigel that no money had been found on Leo's body. "But no one else knew about it!" Daphne said. "At least, I don't think anyone did."

"Obviously, *someone* did, Daphne," I answered.

"Do you think whomever murdered Leo knew about the money, or do you think they found it … afterwards?" she asked.

"I don't know. But I suspect it's an important distinction. Does your father know what you did?" I asked.

Daphne shook her head. "I didn't tell him. I was … I was too ashamed."

"He needs to know. Audrey needs to know as well."

Daphne finished her drink. "I know. I'll tell them."

"Do you want us to come with you?" asked Nigel.

Daphne's face brightened a little, and she nodded. "Would you?"

Nigel said that of course we would. I said nothing. I finished my drink and mulled over what Daphne had told us. I most certainly did not want to accompany her to tell Max and Olive the latest wrinkle in this mess. I could only imagine Olive's wrath at discovering that not only had Daphne taken money from Audrey's trust, but that the money was now gone. It was sure to be ugly. However, at this point, I couldn't figure a way—polite or otherwise—to excuse myself from the scene. So, I did the only thing I could. I got up and headed for the shower.

THIRTY-TWO

"You did *what*?" Olive screamed at Daphne from the throne-like perch of her toile chair later that afternoon.

"I took money from Audrey's account to pay for Leo's silence and for him to go away," Daphne repeated for what must have been the fifth time.

Max stared at Daphne, his expression inscrutable. "*You* did this?"

Daphne glanced at him sharply. "Yes. I just told you that. *I* took out the money and gave it to Leo. And now it's gone."

Max looked as if he was about to say something else, but Audrey spoke first. "Leo really said he'd leave me forever if you paid him?" she asked.

Daphne looked at her, her face pinched with regret. "Yes. I'm sorry, Audrey. I really am. I shouldn't have done it. I was just trying to protect you."

Audrey nodded. "I know. It's okay. You're not to blame. I am. For marrying someone like Leo in the first place."

Max leaned over and took her hand. "Audrey. Please. None of this is your fault. You aren't the first person to make a bad marriage. He took advantage of you. *Leo* is to blame for all of this. And if he weren't already dead ..." Seeing Audrey blanch, he came to an abrupt stop. "Sorry."

Audrey ducked her head. "It's okay. I understand."

Max turned to me. "But what does this mean? For Audrey? Are the police still looking for other leads? Do they really think Audrey could have done this?"

"I don't know," I answered. "I spoke to my friend Marcy and told her about the missing money. I'm sure the police will look into that."

"Could Leo have owed more money to other people?" Daphne asked. "People other than Frank Little?"

"He might have," I said. "Anything is possible."

"Especially where Leo was concerned," said Olive.

Although I hated to admit it, she had a point.

THIRTY-THREE

THE ONE PERSON I thought could answer the question of Leo's debts was Frank. He wasn't at home, so we tried the family restaurant/front. Little's Vittles was a hole in the wall located on a shabby side street on the Lower East Side. The décor was garish. The seating was a mix of red velvet and black pleather. Along the back wall behind the bar were highlights of some of the more famous scenes from Michelangelo's Sistine Chapel. Rather than God's hand reaching out to provide Adam with the spark of life, a muscular version of Danny offered a reclining patron a plate of antipasto. In a nod to the nude Adam and Eve's banishment from Paradise, two would-be patrons were chased out of Little's by a reprimanding hostess. Based on their attire, their crime appeared to be that they were Red Sox fans.

Not surprisingly, the restaurant was not crowded. In fact, the only occupants were Frank and Danny. Frank was wiping down the bar with a questionable-looking dishrag. Danny was sitting on a stool smoking a cigarette and reading the sports page. Neither appeared pleased to see us.

"Landis! What the hell are you doing here?" Danny barked when he saw me.

"I'm a gourmet at heart, Danny. But I am hurt that you can't remember my name. It's Martini. Like the drink." I said.

Danny scoffed. "More like a Shirley Temple," he said.

I smiled. "Why, thank you, Danny."

"I hate Shirley Temples," Danny finished.

"Do have some respect for the dead," Nigel admonished. "That woman cheered up a nation in need."

"Good point. Let's just stick with Martini," I said as I took a seat at the bar. Nigel sat next to me. Skippy merely laid his head on the battered surface and stared at Frank. Nigel and I each picked up one of the menus and read the daily specials.

"We're not open right now," said Frank.

"Well, that is a shame," Nigel said, laying his menu on the bar. "Because you had me with 'The Codfather.'"

"So, have you heard about our mutual friend Leo?" I asked.

Frank nodded. "Yeah. We're all broke up about it."

"I imagine you are. Easy marks with fat bank accounts are hard to come by," I said.

Frank produced a half laugh. Danny glared at him. "What do you want, Martini?" he asked as he stubbed out his cigarette into an ashtray.

"Well, other than a desire to know what exactly is in a vittle, I wondered if Leo might have owed money to anyone besides you?"

Frank cocked an eyebrow. "Man, if that were true then that boy would have been in deep."

"So, is that a no, then?" I asked.

"Yeah. As far as I know, he only owed us. I would have heard about it otherwise. People knew I wanted my money. If there was a ... competition for Leo's attention to that matter, I would know. Why? What did you hear?"

"I ran into Leo the night before he died. He was at The Lucky Lady."

Frank regarded me with wide-eyed amusement. "You were at The Lucky Lady? I would have loved to have seen that."

"I'll be sure to call you next time I go. My point is that when I saw Leo there, he seemed to be in a particularly good mood."

"I'll bet he did," Danny said with a snort.

I glanced at him. "Yes, well he seemed to be in a jolly mood for reasons other than the entertainment." I returned my attention to Frank. "Leo told me that he'd paid off his debt to you. And yet he still had money to fling at the so-called 'lucky ladies' at the club."

Frank met my gaze. "And?" he asked.

"And, I wondered if that was correct? Had Leo paid off his debt?"

Frank nodded. "Yeah. We were all squared up. Why?"

"Well, the last time we chatted, I think someone mentioned something about messing up Leo's smug face. And I think that someone was you. But when I saw Leo that night he was bruise-free, and the next night the only bruising on his face was a result of a disagreement he had with my husband."

Frank and Danny looked at Nigel. Nigel shrugged. "It was a gentlemen's disagreement. I didn't think he was one."

Frank crossed his arms across his chest and frowned. "Yeah. Well, I still planned on smashing his face in, but now that he's dead it seems..."

"Excessive?" suggested Nigel.

Frank nodded and grinned. "Yeah. Excessive. That works."

"But why didn't you, as you so quaintly put it, 'smash his face in' when he paid you back?" I asked.

Frank poured himself and Danny a glass of whiskey from behind the bar. He then held up the bottle to me with a questioning expression. I shook my head no. He shrugged and put the bottle back. "Leo didn't pay me back in person," Frank explained after taking a sip of his drink. "He sent some woman to do it for him. Typical Leo. Always hiding behind a chick."

I frowned. "He sent a woman to pay you? Was it his wife, Audrey?"

"No," said Frank, "It wasn't her."

"So who was it then?"

Frank took another sip and shook his head. "I don't know. I never saw her before. She's not the type of customer we usually get."

"Could she have been one of the dancers from The Lucky Lady?"

Frank laughed at the suggestion. "Not unless they are completely changing their lineup to uptight blondes."

"But she was a friend of Leo's?"

Frank shook his head. "I doubt they were actually friends. She was a scared rabbit. I don't think she was Leo's type. Or visa versa."

"So what did this blonde look like?" I asked.

Frank regarded me in confusion. "I just told you. Blonde."

I sighed. "Yes, but what else? Tall? Thin? Curvy? Sexy? Old? Young?"

Understanding dawned in Frank's eyes. "Oh. Yeah. She was young. Thin. Kind of the Grace Kelly type rather than a Marilyn Monroe, if you know what I mean."

I looked at Frank in surprise. "Why, Frank! I never pegged you for a movie buff."

He nodded. "Only the older stuff. The stuff they put out today is crap."

"A man after my own heart," said Nigel. "Tell me Frank, what does Bogart mean to you?"

Frank regarded him curiously. "What do you mean, what does Bogart mean? Like Humphrey Bogart?"

Nigel nodded.

"Other than being one of the best damn actors of his generation? Nothing. Why, should it?" he asked.

"No. But you've restored my faith that some of greatest actors of our time have not been wholly forgotten."

Frank took another sip of his drink. "One of the greatest love stories, too. That Lauren Bacall was a damn fine woman."

THIRTY-FOUR

NIGEL, SKIPPY, AND I returned to the hotel after our meeting with Frank. I then left the two of them there and paid Marcy a visit. She was sitting with her feet up on her desk and reading a file when I entered her office. Seeing me, she sat up and shut the folder. "Hey, Nic. What's going on?" she asked as she offered me a chair.

"Oh, just the usual Bacchanalia of holiday family dysfunction," I said.

Marcy laughed. "I guess that's one way to put it. Although it's much classier than what I would call it. I guess these high society folks are rubbing off on you."

"God, I hope not," I confessed as I sat down.

"So, what's all this about Leo having a bunch of money on him when he died?" she asked.

"Apparently, he had a bunch of money on him when he died," I answered primly.

Marcy raised an eyebrow. "Something you're not telling me, Nic?"

"Probably," I admitted. "But it's not my thing to tell."

Marcy crossed her arms. "Nic, a man is dead. One of your relatives …"

"One of *Nigel's* relatives," I corrected.

She tipped her head in acknowledgement and started over. "One of *Nigel's* relatives is under suspicion in that death. If you know something that affects this investigation, then I'd appreciate it if you'd share it with me."

"I know, Marcy. And I will. I promise. I just want to make sure that I understand what I think I know before I say anything. I don't want to waste your time investigating a misunderstanding."

Marcy stared at me for a long beat. "Fine, Nic. Have it your way. But I'm warning you. We go back a long way, and I've always counted you as a friend, but that courtesy doesn't extend to your … *Nigel's* … relatives."

"Understood. Don't worry. I'm not going to hide anything from you. I only want to double check some facts first."

"Such as?"

I sighed. "I don't know. Everything. Did you ever get any leads on who killed Fat Saul?"

She shook her head. "No. If anyone knows anything, they aren't talking. I'm not surprised, really. Fat Saul was a psychopath. Maybe whoever killed him is now being hailed as a hero of sorts."

"Or is just the successor to the title."

Marcy gave a wan smile. "That's probably a more likely scenario."

"Do you think either Frank or Danny Little had anything to do with it?" I asked.

Marcy shook her head. "It would make my life so much easier if they had, but honestly, I can't find any evidence linking them to the crime. They both have airtight alibis. And as much as I hate to admit it, they seem legit. Their alibis, not the individuals who provided them, that is."

"Duly noted. What about Lizzy Marks? Any progress there?"

Again Marcy shook her head. She tapped her pen on the manila folder. "We're still keeping an eye on her ex-husband, but there's nothing to connect him to the scene of the crime."

I looked at her in surprise. "What do you mean, there's nothing to connect him? He was practically stalking her."

Marcy nodded. "I know. I know. But technically he obeyed the terms of his restraining order, if not the spirit of it. I can't find anything that puts him in her apartment. Not that I've written him off, of course. I haven't. But until I get something solid, I have to let him go."

"I guess you're right."

Marcy cocked her head and stared at me. "Do you think he had something to do with her death?"

"I don't know. It makes sense on paper, but there's something I'm missing. I still don't get Lizzy and Leo's relationship."

Marcy sat back in her chair and produced a mocking smile. "Really? You don't? I think I have the files from some of our more lascivious cases that might clarify that for you."

"I don't mean *that* part," I said. "I mean, how did they meet? Leo is a … was a gold-digger. Lizzy was cut from the same cloth."

"Seems a match made in heaven, if you ask me."

"But that's just it. It isn't. Leo didn't have any money. Not really. He just had whatever Audrey gave him. And Lizzy didn't have anything either. From what Frank and Danny said, she was good at scamming people, but that's not likely to attract someone like Leo who was looking for a cash cow."

Marcy frowned. "What's your point?"

"I don't know exactly. I just wonder how they met in the first place."

"Does it matter?" she asked.

"I don't know. It might. Any chance I could take a look at the files?"

Marcy let out a reluctant laugh. "You never were lacking for moxie were you, Nic?"

"Moxie? Nope, I've never lacked moxie. Good sense, however, was and always will be a whole other problem."

Marcy pushed two thick folders across her desk. "Well, that goes without saying. Here, I'm going to get a cup of coffee. Would you like one?"

I admitted I did.

"Fine. I'll get you one too. My treat. Why don't you stay here and wait for me? I should only be about twenty minutes. You can hold down the fort while I'm gone."

I smiled at her. "Thanks, Marcy. I owe you."

She nodded. "Remind me one of these days to let you settle up that bill."

———

I started on Lizzy's file first. Elizabeth Marks, a.k.a. "Lizzy," aged forty-seven, was discovered after a concerned neighbor noticed her apartment door was open and investigated. She was pronounced dead at the scene at 6:00 a.m. The coroner concluded that death resulted from a blow to the head. The wound was likely caused from the edge of a chrome side table. Death was instantaneous. Based on the state of the apartment, it appeared that there had been an altercation prior to the attack. The victim's ex-husband, William "Billy" Morgan, was interviewed and released. Bags and boxes found in the victim's bedroom suggested that she was planning on moving. Her landlord, Jerry McLane, confirmed that she had given notice and was scheduled to move out at the end of the month. He knew of no forwarding address.

Although I already knew most of the facts surrounding Fat Saul's case, it helped to read them again too. Saul Washington, a.k.a. "Fat Saul," aged fifty-six, had been found at the Park View Terrace construction site after the foreman, Martin "Marty" White, discovered his body at approximately 5:55 a.m. According to the coroner's report, Fat Saul had been shot twice at close range in the lower abdomen. Death was not instantaneous, and the victim bled out. The coroner estimated the time of death between 12:00 and 3:00 a.m. No one reported hearing any shots. The gun found at the scene was determined to be the gun used in the shooting and was registered to Saul Washington.

I sat back and stared unseeingly at the words. I was missing something. If Fat Saul had gone looking for Leo the night he died, then that meant Leo could have been hiding out at the construction site. But why would he hide out there? And why would he think it would be a safe place?

I decided to have a chat with the owners of Park View Terrace. I moved out of my seat and into Marcy's empty chair. I tapped in a search on Park View Terrace on her computer. Within minutes, I found what I was looking for; the name of the parent company. The name rang a bell. I jotted down the address, scribbled a note to Marcy apologizing for leaving, and left.

———

Park View Terrace was an enormous skyscraper located in Midtown Manhattan. From the looks of the exterior, no expense had been spared; it was fifty stories of sheer glass and concrete reaching skyward. According to large placard outside the site, it would one day house "an exclusive enclave of timeless elegance for people with discerning tastes." I had no idea what that even meant, but I still doubted it. Walking over to a construction worker who appeared to be on a break, I introduced myself as a detective and asked about the recent discovery of a body on the site. As I expected, I was immediately directed to a trailer that served as the main office. I knocked on the door and opened it. It was a nondescript, makeshift kind of office. The décor was early American garage sale. To one side were several beige metal file cabinets and a table covered in blueprints. To the other side was a desk, also made of beige metal. Two empty chairs sat in front of it; one sat behind it. This one was occupied. The woman occupying it looked up at me in irritation. I guessed her to be in her early fifties. Her brown hair was streaked with gray and cut into a sensible bob. Her face was narrow but not unpleasant. A pair of glasses was perched low on her thin nose. "Yes?" she said. "Can I help you?"

"Hello, Detective Landis, NYPD. I need to talk with you about the discovery of the body the other night. That of a Mr. Saul Washington," I said, as I quickly flashed my wallet open. I had made that gesture enough times over the years to know that hardly anyone ever actually looked at the ID. I hoped she would prove to be one of those people. She did.

"Karen Talingo," she said, reaching out to shake my hand. "I already talked to the police," she continued in a polite but firm voice. "And I really am very busy."

"I understand that, and I promise not to take up any more of your time than is necessary," I said as I took a seat in the chair opposite her desk and pulled out the notebook I'd purchased on the way over. "I just have a few questions, Ms. Talingo."

She let out a resigned sigh and sat down. "Fire away."

I nodded. "I understand that one of your crew found the body?" I glanced down at my notebook where I had jotted down the highlights from the file Marcy had shown me. "A Martin White?"

She nodded. "Yes. That's right; Marty found the body on his rounds early that morning. Scared the crap out of him."

I gave a sympathetic smile. "I can well imagine. Did you know the deceased?"

"No," she answered. I scribbled in my notebook.

"Had you ever seen the deceased before?" I asked.

She shook her head. "No. And I never saw him after, either. Marty called the police and then me. By the time I got here, the police had removed the body."

"I see. Now, where was Mr. White when he found the body?"

"He was on one of the upper levels." She paused. "Would you rather talk to Marty?"

I pretended to consider the question. "Perhaps that would be best."

She picked up the phone on her desk and told someone on the other end to send in Marty. After she hung up, she turned to me. "He'll be right down. Can I offer you a cup of coffee?"

I said she could. She fixed us both a cup, and we quietly sipped foul-tasting coffee from Styrofoam cups while we waited for Marty to arrive. Within five minutes there was a knock on the door.

"Come in," called Karen.

The door swung open and a large muscular man with numerous tattoos stepped into the office. "You wanted to see me, Karen?"

She nodded and indicated me. I stood up and offered my hand. "Hello, Mr. White. I'm Detective Landis. I'm just here to follow up on a few things regarding your discovery of the body the other night. It'll only take a minute," I said, indicating the other chair.

Martin nodded, shot an uneasy glance at Karen, and sat down. "I already talked to the police ..." he began.

I smiled and raised my hand. "I know. My boss is just a stickler for paperwork. I swear, it seems like I waste more time writing down stuff that's already been written down, if you know what I mean."

Martin smiled a little and nodded.

I glanced down at my notebook. "So, I have here that you discovered the body?" I glanced back at Martin. He nodded. "And the victim was dead when you found him?"

"Yeah, he was dead all right. I mean, I didn't touch him or anything, but you could tell he was dead."

I nodded sympathetically. "I'm sorry. That must have been a nasty shock."

Martin agreed that it was.

"And where was the victim exactly?"

"On the tenth floor. We're further along on those apartments; the lower ones, I mean. Some of them are almost done."

I nodded. "I see. Could someone have been staying there—maybe a squatter?"

Martin paused. "We do try to keep this place secure at night, but we have had some problems with vagrants; especially now that it's winter. People with no place to go try to find shelter."

Or people who are hiding out from violent loan sharks, I mentally added. "That makes sense," I said. "Did you happen to notice if it looked like someone had been using the apartment for that reason?"

Martin considered the question. "I didn't hang around a long time after I found the body, if you know what I mean. There were some wrappers and stuff around. But it could have been trash from our crew." He looked at Karen sideways. "I mean, they know they're supposed to pick up their trash, but they don't always do it."

"Sure," I said, nodding, "that makes sense. But you did see food wrappers and the like?"

"Yeah. There were empty soda cans and stuff."

"Got it. And did you recognize the deceased?"

Martin shook his head. "No. I never saw the guy before in my life."

I jotted this down and then stood up and smiled at Martin and Karen. "Well, I think that about does it for me. Thank you again. I'm sorry to have bothered you. Hopefully I have all I need for my boss."

Both Karen and Martin stood up. They each appeared relieved that the interview was over.

"Oh, just one more thing," I asked Karen as I glanced at my notebook. "Who owns this site?"

Karen's eyebrows pulled together. "Park View Terrace?" she asked.

"Yes. Who is the owner?"

"Meyers and Company," she answered. "Hang on. I have their card right here. Oh, and here's our brochure if you need more information." She reached into her desk and retrieved both. I took the card, thanked her and Martin, and left.

THIRTY-FIVE

I WAS MAKING MY way back to the hotel when my cell phone rang. It was Marcy. "Where the hell did you go?" she demanded when I answered. "I go and get you a cup of coffee and return to an illegible note and an empty office."

"Would you have preferred a legible note?"

"I'd prefer you not to run off like that. Where did you rush off to anyway?"

"I may have made an unofficial visit to Park View Terrace."

A brief silence followed. "Tell me you didn't."

"Okay. I didn't."

She sighed. "You did, didn't you?"

"I'm not telling you until you make up your mind."

"Never mind. It's probably better that I don't know. Did you learn anything?" she asked.

"Well, according to the brochure I got, the future residents of Park View Terrace will live in 'an atmosphere where elegance and formality reign supreme and enjoy an inherent sense of grandeur and warmth.'"

"What the hell are you talking about?"

"I don't know," I admitted. "It's pretty bad prose."

"Nic?"

"Yes?"

"I'm going to hang up now."

"I can't say I blame you. Thanks again, Marcy."

"Don't mention it. And by that, I mean just what I say. *Don't mention it.*"

―――――

My next visit was to Audrey's. On my way to her apartment, I stopped at a local deli and bought a large container of chicken noodle soup and some sandwiches. Audrey answered on my fifth knock. She was wearing a wrinkled tee shirt and a pair of baggy sweatpants. From their appearance, it seemed that she'd slept in them. Her face was red and blotchy and her hair was matted and tangled. "Oh, hello, Nic," she said her voice dull. "Where's Nigel?"

"He's at the hotel," I answered. "I'm sorry to stop by unannounced, but I wanted to see how you were doing. May I come in for a few minutes? I brought you lunch." I held up the brown bag as evidence.

"Oh, well, okay. Thanks," Audrey said, opening the door wide to let me in. "That was nice of you, but you didn't need to."

"Nonsense," I answered. "You've been through hell. You need to take care of yourself. When did you last eat?"

"Um … yesterday? But I'm not hungry."

"You need to eat something. You sit down. I'll get the plates." Audrey wandered over to the couch and curled up with a large throw pillow while I headed for the kitchen. I found a tray and set out the soup and sandwiches. When I returned to the living room, Audrey was staring into space.

"Here you go," I said, setting the tray down on the table.

Audrey looked blankly at the food. I handed her a spoon. "Eat."

Reluctantly Audrey sat up and began to eat her soup and sandwich. I did the same with mine. Neither of us spoke. After awhile, Audrey pushed her empty plate and bowl away and curled back up on the couch. "Thanks, Nic," she said. "I guess I was hungrier than I realized."

"How are you holding up?"

She shook her head. "It all seems like a nightmare. I keep hoping that I'll wake up and find that this was all a terrible dream."

"I know the feeling," I said.

"But it's not a dream, is it?" she said, her eyes filling with tears. "Leo never loved me. He used me for my money, and I was too stupid to see it. I never thought I'd say this, but I'm glad my parents aren't alive to see what a mess I made of my life."

"I wish I could say something to make you feel better. I'm sorry Leo wasn't a very nice man. But don't beat yourself up over it. You're not the first woman to make a mistake about love."

She sighed and hugged the pillow against her stomach. "I still feel like a fool."

"Well, there's no reason to. Nobody thinks that of you."

She shook her head. "You're just being nice." She paused. "Has there been any news?"

"About Leo's killer?" I asked. Audrey nodded. "No, not really. The police are still investigating. I take it that you didn't see anyone come out of the bathroom before you went in?"

Audrey shook her head. "No one. It was empty when I went in. Only Leo was there."

"I'm sorry. That must have been distressing."

Audrey closed her eyes. "It … it was."

I sat for a moment thinking how to bring up the question I needed answered. There seemed no polite way to do it. "Audrey, I'm sorry to have to ask you this, but there's something that I need to know," I finally said.

Audrey opened her eyes and stared at me with a wary expression. "What?"

"Well, it's about Lizzy Marks."

The wary expression increased. "What about her?"

"Why didn't you tell anyone that she was Max's secretary?"

THIRTY-SIX

THERE WAS A LONG pause. In a dull voice, she said, "How did you find out?"

"Actually, it was just a hunch. But it was a hunch that you just confirmed." Audrey's mouth bunched in anger. I didn't know if it was at me for tricking her or at herself for getting tricked. I didn't care. I pretended not to notice and went on. "I remembered that Lizzy Marks used to be married to a man named Morgan. Lizzy is short for Elizabeth. So is Betty. When Lizzy worked for Max, she used her married name." Audrey stared at me in some confusion. I didn't elaborate. "But that's beside the point," I continued. "What does matter is why didn't you say something."

Audrey looked down. "I couldn't. I didn't want to involve the family any more than they already were. Can you imagine Aunt Olive's reaction if she found out that Leo had been having an affair with Max's secretary?" She shook her head at the thought. "As it stands now, only the police know about Leo's involvement with

Lizzy or whatever her real name was. But if it got out that she once worked for Max, the papers would have a field day."

"Maybe, maybe not. In any case, you should have told the police."

"Does it really matter? She's dead."

"I think it does matter. Quite a bit, actually. Leo met Lizzy when she was working for Max."

"So?"

"So, according to some friends of hers, she found out about an embezzlement scheme at work and was trying to cash in on it. Any idea what it was?"

Audrey looked up at me in surprise. "Embezzlement? At Max's firm?"

"That's what they told me. Mean anything to you?"

Audrey shook her head. "No, nothing."

"Could Leo have been involved?" I asked. "When he came home, you must have asked him where he'd been. What did he tell you?"

"He … he didn't tell me anything really. He said it was none of my damn business what he did."

I stared at her in surprise. "And you just accepted that?"

A spark of anger flashed in her eyes. "Of course not! I was furious, but I couldn't make him tell me where he'd been or what he'd been up to."

"Well, did Leo say anything about his relationship with Lizzy? You knew all about her, you must have brought up the topic. What did he tell you?"

Her eyes focused on the floor. "Nothing really."

I took a deep breath and let it out slowly. "Audrey, I'm trying to help you, but you have to tell me everything you know. Did Leo tell you anything about his relationship with Lizzy?"

Audrey rubbed her hand across her forehead. "When he finally came home, I accused him of having an affair with her. I told him that I knew everything. He just stood there and laughed at me. He said I didn't know anything. He said they were business partners."

"Did he say what this business was?"

"Not really. He said something about a windfall, but that she had double crossed him."

"She'd double crossed him? How?" I asked.

"I don't know. He didn't say. I was too upset to think straight. But … but he said she deserved what she got."

I stared at her. "Audrey, did Leo …?" I let the question hang in the air.

Audrey raised her head, and for the first time, held my gaze. "Yes," she whispered. "He killed her."

"How do you know this?" I asked.

"When I went to her apartment that day, she was on the floor." Audrey closed her eyes at the memory. "I felt for a pulse and, well, there wasn't any. I was about to leave, but I noticed that she had something in her hand." She paused.

"And?" I prompted.

"And it was Leo's cufflink. I know because I gave it to him."

I thought back to the report I'd read in Marcy's office. "I don't recall anything about the police finding a cufflink on the body," I said, hoping that Audrey wasn't about to tell me something stupid.

"That's because I took it," she said, dashing that hope.

"Why on earth would you do that?" I snapped.

Audrey's eyes filled with tears. "I know it was wrong, but I only wanted to protect him! I thought it had to be a mistake of some kind. I thought maybe he'd left his cufflinks there, and she happened to be holding one when she died."

"You can't possibly be that stupid, Audrey."

Audrey brushed away the tears that were starting to slide down her cheeks. "I know. I know. But I saw that cufflink, and I panicked. I grabbed it and ran."

"Did you tell Leo this?"

She nodded. "I did. And I told him that I was done. With him. With our sham of a marriage. I told him I wanted a divorce."

"You did? What did he say?"

"He laughed. He said that I couldn't divorce him. He said that if I tried, he'd go to the police and tell them that *I* had been there too. He said he'd make it look like *I* killed her. Then he thanked me for taking the cufflink. He actually *thanked me*. He said that her death was an accident. That they'd fought, and she came at him or something. He pushed her back and she fell and hit her head."

"He didn't think to call an ambulance?"

Audrey shook her head. "No. He said she died instantly."

"I guess we'll never know, will we? Once he was home, did he call anyone or go anywhere?" I asked.

She shook her head. "No. No one." Audrey gave a loud sniff. "What are you going to do now?" she asked.

"I'm going to find some aspirin," I said, standing up to leave. "And a large bottle of something to chase it down with. I have a feeling I'm going to need it."

THIRTY-SEVEN

I LEFT AUDREY'S APARTMENT, went back to the deli, and bought a large cup of coffee. I sat down at an empty table and tried to think. Although I wasn't surprised to hear that Leo had killed Lizzy, I was surprised that Audrey had tried to cover it up. I had pegged her as having a stronger moral compass than that.

I sipped my coffee and reviewed what I knew. Lizzy had discovered an embezzling scheme at Max's firm and decided to cash in on it. Around that time, Lizzy was discovered to be sleeping with certain clients and was summarily fired. At some point, either before her firing or shortly after it, Lizzy hooked up with Leo. The two of them planned something involving the embezzlement scheme. Before they could finish it, Fat Saul called in his loan, and Leo went into hiding. Someone, possibly a woman, called Fat Saul and revealed where Leo was hiding. Soon after, Fat Saul was found dead from a gunshot wound to the stomach. Lizzy was killed next, and if Audrey's story was true, Leo was the killer. Then Leo blackmailed Daphne to keep quiet about seeing Audrey leave Lizzy's apartment.

He returned home to Audrey and attended her birthday party only to wind up dead in the men's room.

I drank some more coffee. The story didn't make sense. If Leo had killed Lizzy then why would he hang around her apartment to see who else showed up? He wouldn't. He couldn't have been there when Audrey arrived. And why would Leo go to Daphne with his blackmail proposition? Again, he wouldn't. He'd go to Max or even Audrey herself. Pieces of the puzzle started to fit together.

I finished my coffee and decided to pay Daphne a visit. She answered my knock, seemingly surprised not only to find me on her doorstep, but alone. Her face appeared paler than usual, and there were dark circles under her eyes.

"Nic," she said with a forced smile, "this is a surprise! Come on in. Is everything all right?"

"That depends on your definition of all right," I said as I followed her into her living room. I took a seat on one couch while she sat on the opposite one.

"Can I get you a drink?" she asked, her smile still in place. "Coffee? Something stronger?"

"No, thank you. I came by to ask you about one of your clients."

Her smile dimmed. "Oh, really? Which one?"

"Meyers and Company."

She sat back in her chair and crossed her legs. "Yes? What about them?" she asked with just the right note of casual interest.

"Well, just an interesting tidbit I learned about them. The man who was looking for Leo—Fat Saul? I believe I told you about him?"

Daphne nodded hesitantly.

"Well, as you know, he was found dead a few days back. I don't know if I mentioned this, but his body was found at the Park View

Terrace construction site." I paused to see if she was going to make this easy or difficult. She said nothing. Difficult it was, then.

"Do we really have to play cat and mouse, Daphne? You know as well as I do that Park View Terrace is owned by none other than your client, Meyers and Company."

She flushed. "Well, what of it? It doesn't have anything to do with *me*. I had nothing to do with that man's death! Fat Saul was a thug! A violent thug! You told me that yourself!"

"Yes, I know I did. I fed you all the information you needed, didn't I? You played that rather neatly. You needed to find Leo, and so you set me on the case. But you never wanted Leo to come home to Audrey's waiting arms. Once you found out about Fat Saul— who I so helpfully told you was a violent thug—you called him, didn't you?"

Daphne's face went very white. "Me? Don't be absurd. Why would I call this Fat Saul person?"

"Simple. So you could tell him where to find Leo. You told him that Leo was hiding out at the Park View Terrace construction site, and you sent him there hoping that Fat Saul would take care of Leo for you. It must have been a nasty shock for you when I told you that it was Fat Saul's body that was found at the site and not Leo's."

Daphne's pupils shrunk to angry black dots. She pressed her lips together until they were hard white lines. "This is absurd," she spit out. "What you are saying makes no sense. Leo was a worthless ass, but that doesn't mean I wanted him dead. Audrey was the one married to him, not me."

"Yes, but *you* were the one he was blackmailing."

Daphne's face registered relief. She even laughed a little. "But I told you about that! He said he'd go to the police about Audrey unless I paid him!"

"I'm talking about before that."

She affected an expression of confusion. "Before that?"

"Yes. *Before* that. The first time I visited your apartment, Skippy got into your trash. Among the things I fished out of his mouth were Werther's candy wrappers. The same candy that Audrey stocks for Leo. I didn't think anything about it at the time, but later I wondered if Leo had been here. And if he had, why? Then I found out that there were rumors of an embezzlement scheme at your firm. It was you, wasn't it? You were the one taking money out of Audrey's account, and Leo found out about it. I'm guessing Lizzy Marks cued him into that."

"Lizzy Marks?" Daphne repeated, as if confused.

"We can refer to her as Betty Morgan, if you'd prefer. Your father's ex-secretary. The one you had fired for sleeping with the clients. Let me hazard a guess on this. She slept with the man you were seeing, yes?" Daphne flushed an ugly shade of red. "When you found out about it, you had her fired. That didn't sit well with her. When I talked to her, she seemed to have a beef with your family that I found hard to explain. But then I remember she said something about you all having your hand in the till just like everyone else. I can only imagine that she was referring to *you*."

"She was a greedy slut!" Daphne bit out, no longer bothering to pretend. I was grateful for the honesty. "Yes, she slept with my boyfriend. And yes, I had her sorry ass fired!"

I didn't bother pointing out that her boyfriend was just as much to blame, if not more so. "And so she decided to get you back," I said. "Why did you take money out of the account in the first place? Need some new shoes?"

She glared at me. "Don't be ridiculous. I didn't do it for personal gain. I'm not like that. I made … I made a mistake on a case. I screwed up a settlement for one of our clients. If it was discovered it would be malpractice. I could have lost my license. So, I … I dipped into Audrey's account to cover the cost. I was going to pay it back. I swear."

"Uh-huh," I said, not caring if that was true or not. "So, then what happened?"

Her face grew angry. "That slime ball Leo shows up, telling me that unless I pay him, he's going to tell everyone what I did. I figured out that it was Betty who must have tipped him off. I told him that I didn't have the money; that I needed a few days. He said that was fine, but that he needed to lay low until then. He said he owed some people money. I told him about Park View Terrace. I know all the access codes there. He was going to go there while I came up with the money."

"But then I came along and told you about Fat Saul."

She nodded sheepishly. "Something like that."

"After you found out that it was Fat Saul who was looking for Leo, you thought you could tip off Saul and kill two birds with one stone. Too bad for you that Leo managed to get the jump on Saul. Of course, it turned out worse for Saul."

"You have to believe me," she said, suddenly pleading. "I was desperate! I just wanted Leo gone. From Audrey's life and from mine. I wasn't thinking. I didn't mean for him to die. I just thought this Fat Saul guy would scare him away for good."

I didn't know whether I believed her. I almost didn't care. "So what happened when Leo came out of hiding?" I asked.

"He called me and told me that my time was up, and I needed to pay him his money," she said.

"When was this?" I asked.

"The day before he came home to Audrey."

"And I imagine that you had to dip once again into Audrey's trust fund to cover the bill. Poor thing, I hope you left *something* for her."

A crimson stain crept across Daphne's cheeks. "Yes. I took the money from her trust. What else was I supposed to do?"

"I can think of at least ten better options right off the bat, but there's no point in reviewing those now. So you took the money, and then what?" Before she could answer, I held up my hand and said, "Wait, let me guess. Leo told you to take it to Frank Little."

Daphne glanced at me in surprise. "Yes. How did you know that?"

"I talked with Frank Little. He described you pretty accurately. Said a nervous, uptight blonde had dropped off the money. That sounds like you, wouldn't you say?"

Daphne nodded. "It was horrible," she said, shuddering at the memory. "Those men are thugs."

I leaned back in my chair and crossed my legs. "That may be true. But at least *they* are up front about what they are."

Daphne's eyes narrowed. "What's that supposed to mean?"

"Seriously? *That* was too subtle?"

She pressed her lips together and looked away. "Okay. Maybe I deserved that."

"Oh, you deserve that and much more, I'd say. So, when did you figure out that Betty Morgan and Lizzy Marks were the same person?" I asked.

Daphne didn't answer right away. "I don't think I want to talk to you any more about this."

"Too bad. I've got a terrible headache, and I'm not in the mood for games. Now, when did you figure it out? Was it when I mentioned the fact that Lizzy Marks was a blonde in her forties with butterfly tattoos on her ankle? Because, I have to suspect that that little description might have tipped you off."

Daphne flushed, but at least she didn't deny it. "It's true. When you told me that, I figured that they had to be the same person."

Another piece of the puzzle slid into place. "You went to her apartment, didn't you? You went there to confront her. What happened? Did you kill her?"

"No!" Daphne's eyes were wide with fear. "I didn't! I swear to you! I went there, yes. But only to talk to her; to try and get her to see reason."

"What happened? Did she see reason?"

Daphne frowned. "No. She didn't. She was horrible. She said *I* was horrible and that she would be happy to ruin me even if there wasn't any money to be made. We exchanged some choice words, but when I left she was very much alive. I swear to you she was alive!"

"And I'm guessing that when you left you were seen by none other than Leo."

Daphne nodded. "Yes. He saw me. How did you know that?"

"It didn't make sense that Leo would go to *you* if he'd seen Audrey leave Lizzy's apartment. If he wanted to blackmail anyone, he'd go to Max. But it did make sense that he'd go to you if he saw *you*."

Daphne looked down at her hands. "You're right. Leo called me the day of the party and told me that he'd seen me leaving the apartment, and unless I paid him *again*, he'd go to the police."

"Lord, but you are easy to blackmail. Didn't it occur to you that he had a hell of a reason for killing Lizzy himself?"

She looked at me in confusion. "No. Why would he want to kill her? Weren't they partners?"

"They were, but Leo must have realized that Fat Saul didn't stumble across him by accident. He knew that someone had tipped him off. It didn't occur to him that it was you—he'd never mentioned Fat Saul to you and figured you'd have no way of finding out about him. The only other person who knew where he was hiding and his trouble with Fat Saul was Lizzy."

Daphne paled. "So Leo went there to kill Lizzy?"

I shrugged. "I have no idea. But I imagine that if he wasn't suspicious of her before, he was after seeing you leave the apartment. Maybe he thought you two had formed a new arrangement. One that didn't include him."

Daphne considered this, her eyes wide. "Oh, my God. I was furious with her, but I didn't want her to die. Do you really think that seeing me there sealed her fate?"

I raised an eyebrow. "That's a little dramatic, don't you think? No, I think Lizzy sealed her own fate when she took up blackmailing people with lowlifes like Leo. Now, about the money that you said you gave Leo the night he was killed. There never was any money, was there?"

Daphne bit her lip. "What do you mean?"

"I mean that you never gave him any money, did you? You just said you did so you could have an excuse as to why all that money is missing from Audrey's trust. Am I right?"

She looked as if she were going to deny it, but thankfully didn't. She let out a half sigh and half moan and sank back into the couch. After a minute, she said, "Does … does Audrey know any of this?"

"You mean how you were helping yourself to her money?" Daphne blanched at my choice of words. I didn't care. I shook my head. "No. Not yet. But she will. And if you have a shred of decency left, you'll do it yourself."

She nodded. "I will. I just hope she can forgive me."

"Considering what she put up with from Leo, I think she will. She seems to have a very high threshold for tolerating and forgiving rotten behavior."

Daphne dropped her head into her hands. "Oh, God. I'm a horrible person. Betty was right. What have I done? You must hate me."

I let out a sigh of my own and stood up. "I don't hate you, Daphne. I don't like you very much right now, but I don't hate you. I think you should be more worried about how you are going to explain all of this to your parents and Audrey. If I were you, I'd worry about *them*, not me. Now, if you'll excuse me, I am late for a date with a tall glass of something alcoholic."

Daphne stood up as well. She offered me her hand. "Thank you, Nic. I hope that one day you can forgive me and we can be friends."

I shook her hand. "Sure," I said and then turned to go.

"Wait," she said in a nervous voice. "Aren't you going to ask me if I killed Leo?"

I turned around and looked at her. "Not today, Daphne. I've had about all I can take of this case for one day. Why don't we leave that question for tomorrow?"

I left her standing in her foyer, her face lined with worry.

THIRTY-EIGHT

IT WAS LATE AFTERNOON by the time I got back to the hotel. Nigel had ordered room service and was liberally sharing it with Skippy. They were both lying on the bed watching Hitchcock's *North by Northwest*. Seeing me, Skippy let out a happy bark, jumped off the bed, and ran to me, wagging his tail. Nigel remained on the bed, his eyes fixed on the screen.

"Well, it's nice that *one* of you is glad to see me," I said as I rubbed Skippy's ears.

"Shhh," Nigel replied. "This is one of my favorite parts."

"The whole *movie* is your favorite part," I countered as I crawled onto the bed next to him. Skippy jumped up as well and snuggled against me. I turned my attention to the TV screen. Cary Grant and Eva Marie Saint were suggestively bantering back and forth over dinner on the train. "I love this part," said Nigel. "Right here, where Eva Marie Saint says that she 'never discusses love on an empty stomach.' Watch her mouth. The censors dubbed her line. What she originally said was, 'I never make love on an empty stomach.'"

"Speaking of which," I said, "pass me some of that chicken."

———

Later, I told Nigel about my discoveries. "I'm sorry, but I'm going to have to call Marcy and bring her up to date," I said as I brushed the tangles out of my hair.

Nigel glanced at me in confusion. "Why would you be sorry? *You* didn't do anything."

"I know. But it's not going to be pleasant for your family. I doubt we'll ever get another Christmas card from your Aunt Olive again."

Nigel grabbed my hand and gave it a reassuring squeeze. "Darling, Aunt Olive doesn't send us Christmas cards *now*."

"You know what I mean."

"I do. But don't worry about it." His expression grew somber. "Aunt Olive may never thank you properly for all you've done, but I hope you know that I appreciate it. And so does everyone else."

I smiled at him. "Thanks."

He nodded. "Just don't do anything dangerous. I couldn't live with myself if anything happened to you."

"Don't tell me that you've gotten fond of me," I teased.

Nigel's expression remained grave. "I'm serious, Nic. Promise me that you'll be careful."

I kissed him lightly on the mouth. "I promise."

He kissed me back. Giving me a searching look as if to verify my promise, he finally nodded as if satisfied with what he saw. "Okay. Now, go and call Marcy."

Marcy wasn't surprised to hear what I'd learned. "We found out that Lizzy had once worked for Max's firm, too. I just got confirmation an hour or so ago. That led us to check into the construction site as well. So, Daphne was the one who told Leo to hide out there, huh?"

"Yes. Once she discovered that Fat Saul was looking for Leo, she led him straight to Leo."

"Where we are to assume that Leo killed him?"

"It would seem so."

"And what about what Audrey told you? Do you believe that Leo killed Lizzy as well?"

"I do, actually. I think he thought his big plan to get all that money was crumbling, and he lashed out."

"It does have a ring of truth to it," she conceded. "The problem is that he's dead. Supposed confessions from dead people rarely go over well with the DA."

I sighed. "I know. What are you going to do now?"

"I'm going to take all this to Tom Cutter. It's in his hands as to what happens next. But listen, Nic. There's something you should know. The lab came back with the results on the knife. The only prints on it were Audrey's."

"People have been known to wear gloves, Marcy."

"I know, Nic. But I think you should be prepared for ... well, just be prepared."

I didn't ask her for what. I think I already knew.

Two hours later, Max called to tell us that Audrey had been arrested for Leo's murder. Nigel asked him if he wanted us to come over. He did. Olive had become hysterical at the news, and Max had finally been forced to give her a generous dose of Valium. She was now sleeping.

By the time Nigel and I arrived at their apartment, Olive's status had changed from "sleeping" to "resting comfortably." She sat glassy eyed in her usual chair. She produced a vague smile upon seeing us. Daphne was also in attendance. She sat on the couch near her mother. She ducked her head in embarrassment when she saw me.

"How are you holding up, Aunt Olive?" Nigel asked as he bent down to give her a kiss on her check.

Olive produced a loopy smile. "You're a handsome devil," she said. "What's your name?"

Nigel frowned. "It's me, Aunt Olive. Nigel. Are you all right?"

She smiled again. "I'm just kidding. Don't worry about me, Nigel dear," she said, her voice slow and a little thick. "We need to focus on Audrey. We need to make the police understand that she didn't kill Leo." Turning to me, she stretched out her hand and took hold of mine. "Nic? Can you do that? Can you make the police see reason?" She raised pleading eyes to mine.

Shocked that she'd actually called me Nic rather than Nicole, I didn't respond right away. "I'm doing my best, Olive. I can promise you that," I finally said.

She nodded. "I know you will, dear. You're a good person. And you really are very pretty. Even when your hair was short. I'm so sorry about all of this. But they'll see. She didn't kill him. She didn't." She leaned her head back against the chair. Skippy sat down next to her and rested his head on the arm of her chair. She smiled at him and began to stroke his fur. "Nice doggie," she murmured before closing her eyes.

I looked to Nigel in mild alarm. Nigel turned to Max. "How much Valium did you give her?" he whispered. "She's gonzo!"

"Trust me, this is preferable to what she was like before," said Max. "I've never seen her so upset. It was torture to see her in so much pain."

"Well, she's definitely numb now," said Nigel, looking back at Olive. She was still petting Skippy, her eyes closed and a faraway look on her face.

"Can I get you something to drink?" Max asked. "Coffee? Soda?"

"Stop when you get to scotch, and then I'll have it neat," said Nigel.

Max gave a faint smile. "Done. And what can I get for you, Nic?"

"I'll have the same. Thanks, Max."

Max left to make the drinks. Nigel and I sat down. Daphne said nothing. Olive remained with her head back and her eyes closed. It sounded as if she were faintly humming. Then she started to sing, her voice soft and low. "Oh, I'd hate to live in Jersey," she crooned. "And I'll tell you the reason why. A fellow got hit with a bag of shit, and some got in his eye." No one spoke. Olive resumed humming. Skippy moved away from her and sat next to me. He rested his head on my lap. I laid a reassuring hand on his back.

"So, where is Joe today?" I asked, if only to break the awkward silence.

"It's *Joseph*, goddammit!" Olive muttered, her eyes still closed. Everyone ignored her.

"Mother gave him the day off. She didn't want him to know what was going on," Daphne replied while staring at the floor.

"What's being done about Audrey?" Nigel asked.

"Toby is trying to arrange a bail hearing. Dad was going to do it, but Mother became hysterical, and he couldn't leave her." Daphne glanced at Olive in irritation. "It was quite unlike anything I've ever seen."

"How was Audrey?" I asked.

Daphne shrugged. "Numb, I think. She talked to Dad, though, not me."

I nodded. "Have you told them what you told me?"

She nodded at the floor. "Yes. They know."

Max returned with our drinks. "So, Toby is trying to get bail set for Audrey?" I asked.

"Yes," said Max. "I talked to him a little while ago. He's fairly confident that he can arrange something. He's going to call me when he knows more."

"Daphne said you talked to Audrey. How is she?" Nigel asked.

"She's holding up all right, I suppose. I don't think the reality of it has sunk in yet. I hope to have her out of jail before it does. She's never been a particularly strong person." Max turned tired eyes to me. The lines on his face seemed more pronounced than they were yesterday. "Daphne told me about her role in all of this, Nic. I'm sorry that you were ever asked to be involved in this whole sordid mess. I really am. I'm heartily ashamed."

The sound of a half sob escaped from Daphne. I ignored her.

"It's all right, Max," I said. "That's what family is for. We are all privy to each other's worst secrets."

Max twisted his mouth into a half smile. "True. But in our case, it seems that some family secrets are more atrocious than others."

Nigel scoffed. "Max, we're hardly the Borgias. Yes, Daphne took money that wasn't hers to cover up a screwup at work. And, yes, Audrey not only didn't tell the police about finding Lizzy's body, but also failed to mention that Lizzy used to work for you. But those are human failings. They aren't the first people to exercise bad judgment."

Daphne kept her head low. "You forgot to add in the part where I sent a known thug to where Leo was hiding. I'm responsible for that man's death," she said.

"No, *Leo* is," Nigel corrected. "I'm not saying that you deserve a merit badge, Daphne, but let's be honest. By all accounts, Fat Saul was a violent thug who probably did a lot of very bad things in his life. Leo, as we've learned, was something of a sociopath. He most likely killed Fat Saul and Lizzy. There are some who might say that the world isn't really too worse off for both their passings. I'm not trying to diminish what you did, but I think we need to keep it in perspective."

Daphne raised her head and shot Nigel a grateful smile. Seeing her father's stern, disappointed face, her smile vanished. "Dad, please forgive me," she said, her voice low. "I am so sorry. I know it was wrong. When I realized that I'd screwed up the settlement, I panicked. All I could think of was that I didn't want to get disbarred. I didn't want to disappoint you."

Max was unmoved. "And yet, that's exactly what you did," he said, his voice harsh. "I raised you to be better than that."

Daphne lowered her head again. Max glowered. I sipped my drink and scratched Skippy behind his ears.

THIRTY-NINE

An hour or so later, Toby called to say that he was pretty sure he could get Audrey out on bail, but that Max needed to come downtown to sign some papers. Nigel and I left Daphne to look after Olive and returned to the hotel. Not feeling very sociable, we ordered room service. While we waited for it to arrive, Nigel made us a drink.

"So what do you thing will happen to Audrey?" Nigel asked as he handed me my glass.

I took a sip. "I have no idea. Obviously, she'll be well defended, but I don't know about the rest of it."

Nigel sat next to me on the loveseat. He put his arm around my shoulder and took a sip from his glass. Skippy curled up at our feet. "Do you think she might have actually done it?" he asked.

"She might have," I said. "Lord knows if *I* were married to him, I'd want to kill him."

"If *you* were married to him, *I'd* kill him," said Nigel, giving me a kiss.

I smiled. "You say the nicest things, Mr. Martini."

———

We awoke the next morning to the peal of the telephone. Nigel answered it. "Oh, hi, Marcy," he said. "Yes, she's right here. Hang on." He handed me the phone.

"Hello?" I said.

"Hi, Nic," said Marcy. "Sorry to call so early, but I thought you'd want to hear this." I glanced at the alarm clock. It was 8:05.

"No problem. What's up?"

"Well, just when I thought this case couldn't get any weirder, it did. We got the autopsy report on Leo this morning. Guess what he died from?"

"I assumed that it was from the stab wounds."

"Well, you'd be wrong."

I sat up. "You mean he wasn't murdered?"

"Oh, no," she said. "He was murdered all right. But it was poison, not a knife that killed him."

"Poison!" I repeated. Nigel looked at me and mouthed the word "What?" I held up a finger indicating for him to wait a minute. "What kind of poison?" I asked.

"Right now, it looks like hemlock."

"Hemlock!" Nigel's eyes opened wide. "Dear God. What does this mean for Audrey?" I asked.

"I don't know for sure. But, even if Audrey stabbed Leo, I don't see how she could be charged for murder since the knife didn't kill him. Anyway, I just thought you'd want to know. I'll keep you posted."

I thanked Marcy and turned to Nigel. "Leo was poisoned," I told him. "With hemlock, apparently. He was already dead when he was stabbed."

Nigel let out a low whistle. "Are they going drop the charges against Audrey?"

"Marcy didn't say. But, I would imagine they are going to have to dig around a little more before they home in on a suspect. The fact that he was poisoned widens the circle of possible candidates."

Nigel shook his head. "Leave it to Leo to get murdered twice."

———

Nigel called Daphne to tell her the news. She seemed just as surprised as we were. She said she would call Max and then call us back. Nigel and I got dressed and ordered room service. While we waited for it to arrive, Max called.

"Is it true?" he asked. "Did someone poison Leo?"

"That's what the coroner thinks," I said. "I'm not sure what this does for Audrey, but I have to imagine it helps."

"I agree. I'm going to call the DA now and see what they think. If there's a God, maybe we can get the charges dropped and put an end to this."

"I hope they drop the charges, but this latest development hardly puts an end to it, Max. The police are still going to want to know who poisoned Leo," I said.

"Oh, I know, but I think we can make a valid case that one of Leo's more unsavory acquaintances had a hand in that. That Frank Little man, for instance."

I made a noncommittal response and asked Max to keep us posted. He promised he would and then hung up. I held the phone in my hand for a moment thinking. Then I asked Nigel to find me Janet Harris's phone number.

FORTY

By late afternoon, Audrey had been released. The DA had not yet decided if he was going to pursue his case against her, but Max was confident that it was only a matter of time before he dropped all charges. In the meantime, Audrey had surrendered her passport and promised not to leave town.

Olive was overjoyed at the news. She hugged Audrey fiercely and sobbed with relief when she saw her. We had all gathered at Max's for Audrey's homecoming. Audrey appeared pale and almost in shock. "So, Leo was poisoned?" she asked us.

I nodded. "That's what the coroner thinks."

Audrey looked at me in disbelief. "This is all so surreal. I feel as if I'm in a dream. Well, more of a nightmare really."

Olive patted her hand. "I know, dear. But the worst is over. You'll see. You will be happy again. You will be strong again. You will be *you* again."

Audrey looked down at her hands. She twisted her wedding ring a few times and then removed it, placing it on the table in front of her. Skippy moved toward her and laid his head on her lap. Audrey smiled at him and began to pet his head. "I hope so," she said. "I'd like to think that will happen. I don't like who I became when I was with Leo. I was so obsessed with making him happy that I didn't notice how miserable I was. I let myself get lost along the way."

Olive clutched Audrey's hands in hers. Skippy gave her a baleful look at the loss of her attention. "You don't know how happy it makes me feel to hear you say that, my dear," she said. "I know it's been a terrible time for you, but maybe now the fog is finally lifting. Maybe now you'll be able to once again see things clearly."

Daphne had been sitting quietly on the couch, nervously chewing at her fingernails. She now said, "Audrey? I just want you to know how ashamed I am for what I did. I never should have taken money from your account. When I think about everything that's happened, I can't help wondering if it all could have been avoided had I just been honest. I'm so, so sorry."

Audrey produced a faint smile. "It's okay, Daph. I understand. When you're desperate you do desperate things. If anyone understands that, it's me. Look at me. I removed evidence that Leo had killed that woman. I sat back and did nothing while he tried to blackmail you. I was so worried about how we appeared that I lost sight of myself. I lost sight of what's right. I just want you all to know that I appreciate you sticking by me. And I promise, I will never lose myself again."

"We're family, Audrey," said Max with a kind smile. "We stick by one another, good times and bad. The important thing is that you are home. And that calls for a drink. What can I get everyone?"

Orders were duly placed, and Toby offered to help Max fill them. When they left the room, Olive whispered to Audrey, "Now, *there's* a young man you can count on."

Daphne rolled her eyes, "Subtle, Mother. Very subtle."

Audrey smiled. "Toby is amazing, and I'd be very lucky if he cared for me, but I don't think he thinks of me that way, Aunt Olive."

It was Olive's turn to roll her eyes. "Then you're blind, my dear. That man adores you. He'd marry you in heartbeat. You've been given a second chance at love. Take it."

Audrey looked quizzically at Olive and then toward the doorway where Toby had just exited with Max. For the first time this week, her expression was almost hopeful.

Next to me, Nigel muttered in a low voice only I could hear, "Call me old-fashioned, but maybe she should bury the first husband first."

FORTY-ONE

IT WAS LATE BY the time Nigel and I returned to our hotel. There was a message at the front desk from Janet Harris. She had returned my call. I hadn't given her my cell phone number. I wanted to make sure I was alone when I took her call. I glanced at my watch and saw that it was too late to call her back. It would have to wait until morning. Which was just as well; I suspected I wasn't going to like what she had to tell me.

Nigel took off his blazer when we got back to our room and flung it on the bed. Skippy stared mournfully at the occupied space. "I'm making a drink," he said. "Would you like one?"

"Yes, please," I answered as I retrieved his coat and hung it up in the closet. Skippy jumped up onto the vacated spot and settled in. I opted for the chair. Nigel returned with my drink and sat in the other chair.

"Cheers," he said as he clinked his glass against mine.

"Back 'atcha," I replied.

"I have one quick housekeeping item that we need to go over," he said as he stretched his legs onto the ottoman.

"I'm all ears," I replied, taking a sip.

He produced an exaggerated leer. "Don't sell yourself short, sweetheart. What I wanted to talk to you about is this; as you know, we are scheduled to return home tomorrow."

"This is true."

"However, I suspect that we aren't, are we?"

I took another sip. "Is that going to be a problem?" I asked.

He looked at me, his expression somber. "I don't know, is it?"

"That depends on what Janet Harris has to tell me," I said.

Nigel nodded and stared at his shoes. "That's what I was afraid you were going to say."

"I don't have to ask her, you know. We can just leave as planned if you'd prefer."

Nigel looked at me and smiled. "I appreciate the offer. But I think I'd feel a little dirty if we did that." He paused. "And not in the good way."

"Well, we can't have that," I said.

"To Janet Harris," he said, clinking my glass again.

"To Janet Harris," I repeated.

FORTY-TWO

I CALLED JANET HARRIS first thing the next morning. It wasn't a
very long conversation, but she told me what I needed to know. My
next call was to Frank Little. I explained to him that I wanted to
rent out his restaurant for dinner that evening and why his coop-
eration was necessary.

"This ain't going to jeopardize Danny's probation, is it?" he asked.

"It shouldn't. I'll make sure Detective Garcia knows everything,"
I promised. "Danny's involvement shouldn't be an issue."

He paused, and then said, "Fine. We have a deal. I'll have everything ready for you for seven o'clock."

I thanked him and hung up. Then I called Marcy while Nigel
called his family. When all the calls were made, Nigel made us each
a very strong Bloody Mary. Then we went back to bed for an hour.

———

By late afternoon all was ready. I'd arranged for a limo to ferry all
of us to the restaurant. Everyone piled in and the mood was almost

celebratory. Even Olive was pleased by my efforts until the limo pulled up in front of Little's Vittles. "*This* is where you are taking us to eat?" she asked me, her voice horrified.

When I answered that it indeed was, her face grew pale. She pulled out her purse and rummaged through it for her pills. Taking one, she closed her eyes as if to speed up the effects.

Nigel got out first and helped everyone out of the car. "How did you ever find this place?" Toby asked me once he was on the street.

"An old acquaintance runs it," I answered.

Toby shot a dubious glance at the glowing neon sign. "I see. Is it Zagat-rated?" he asked.

"Oh, I don't think so," I answered. "Speaking of which, I'd avoid the veal."

Toby looked at me in some alarm before taking Audrey's arm and escorting her to the entrance. Nigel ushered Max, Olive, and Daphne in while Skippy and I brought up the rear. Danny was waiting at the door for us, his expression truculent. "Good evening, Mrs. Martini," he said upon seeing me. "We have your table ready."

I smiled brightly. "Why, thank you, Danny," I said. "I'm sure everything will be up to your usual standards."

Danny looked at me suspiciously. "What the hell is that supposed to mean?" he asked.

"Just what it does," I replied. "Oh, and Danny?"

He turned his head and regarded me with faint irritation. "What?"

"Before I forget. If you ever call my hotel room, house, apartment, or cell phone for that matter and threaten me again, I will personally see that both your knees are broken beyond repair." I ended my statement with a smile.

227

Danny's expression of irritation quickly morphed into one of surprise. "How did you …" He made a lame attempt to deny it. "What are you talking about?"

"Don't even try it, Danny. I know it was you who called me the other morning. Normally I wouldn't make a big fuss, but Mr. Martini is very particular about his beauty sleep. Now, here's my last piece of advice to you," I leaned in close. "Whatever underhanded scheme you have going on here at this place, I'd end it right now. Because my friend Marcy, or as you know her, Detective Garcia, will sniff it out and before you know it, you'll be right back in prison with a full dance card."

Danny blinked at me. I smiled. A thin young man wearing a white waiter's jacket and sporting a large Adam's apple approached our group and beckoned for us to follow him the table. As we did, another man approached and tapped me on my arm. He was tall and fleshy with light sandy hair fashioned into a doubtful combover. "Mrs. Martini?" he asked.

I admitted that I was. He produced a rather oily smile, and I suddenly recognized him. "You're Flynn Sawyer, aren't you? The lawyer?"

He smiled, pleased at my recognition. "Yes, that's correct. I represent Mr. Little here," he said, indicating Danny.

"I see," I answered. "Congratulations. I'm sure he's a very lucrative client."

Danny produced a growling noise. I ignored him.

"Well," Flynn replied. "I want to make sure that you understand that I am here to see that Mr. Little's rights are not violated."

"Oh, please," I said with a scoff, "the only thing in danger of being violated tonight is my digestive system. Besides, Danny and I understand each other. Don't we, Danny?" Danny jerked his head into a semblance of a nod. "Now, if you'll excuse me," I said, "I need to attend to my guests."

Danny and Flynn went to the bar and took a seat, while Nigel and I made our way to the table. As I'd arranged, we were the restaurant's only customers. "I just want to take a moment again to thank everyone for joining Nigel and me for our last night out in New York. I know it's been a difficult week."

There were muted sounds of greetings and a few uneasy glances. I took a seat at one end of the table, while Nigel sat opposite me at the other end. The waiter passed around menus and took our drink orders. Olive's eyes grew wide as she read the dinner options. She reached for her purse and downed another pill.

Max cleared his throat and said, "Well, thank you for inviting us all out to dinner, Nigel and Nic. It was very kind of you." His voice trailed off as his gaze met with the image of Danny àla God on the back wall.

I smiled. "Thank you. Nigel and I wanted to get everyone together one last time before we head home. It's been a hellish week for everyone, especially Audrey." Everyone now turned to Audrey, who ducked her head awkwardly. "Nigel and I thought that maybe tonight could provide a little closure." Next to her, as always, was Toby. He patted her hand in a comforting gesture. Hearing my words, he glanced at me sharply.

"What do you mean by closure?" he asked.

"An end. A conclusion." I clarified.

"I don't think there's any need for that," Max said. "Leo is dead, and Audrey needs to move forward, not dwell in the past."

"I quite agree," I said, "but I don't think that anyone will be able to move on until Leo's killer is identified. Otherwise a cloud of suspicion will always follow Audrey."

"Yes, but that's for the police to determine," said Olive, her voice unnaturally calm. "There's no need for you to get involved. Unless you're saying that you know who killed Leo."

"Well, that's just it," I said. "I do."

FORTY-THREE

No one spoke. From the other end of the table, Nigel gave me an encouraging nod to continue. I took a deep breath and did so. "As most of you now know, Leo owed a great deal of money to a man named Fat Saul. When Fat Saul decided to call in the entire loan, Leo found himself in a tight spot. He didn't have the money and although he knew that Audrey would get it for him if he asked, the amount was so large that she would need Max and Olive to approve the withdrawal. He rightly assumed that they would never agree to such a thing." I paused as the waiter returned with our drink orders. No one else spoke. They all seemed very intent on taking a sip of their drinks.

The waiter gave a nervous cough and said, "Can I make you an offer you can't refuse?"

Everyone turned to him in confusion. "Excuse me?" I finally asked.

He coughed again nervously and explained. "Um … it's what I'm supposed to say before I tell you about the appetizer specials."

I stared at him for a beat, and then turned to where Danny was sitting at the bar. "Really?" I asked. "*Really?*"

Danny just shrugged. I turned back to the waiter. "Okay. Let's hear them."

He coughed again. "We have A Salt and Battery Fish and Chips…"

"Done," said Nigel. The waiter looked at Nigel in confusion. "There's also the You Won't Be Sorry Calamari," he continued.

"We'll have both of those," I said. He nodded and headed to the kitchen. I paused and took a sip of water. "Now, as it happened, Leo had gotten … friendly … with a woman named Lizzy Marks," I continued. "Lizzy also went by the name Betty Morgan, who, as you all know, used to work for Max." Everyone turned to look at Max. "When Daphne found out that Betty had been sharing her favors with various clients, including one that Daphne was seeing, Daphne had her fired." They now turned their attention to Daphne. I took another sip of water. "Unfortunately for Daphne, Betty knew something rather damning about Daphne. She knew that Daphne had helped herself to some of Audrey's trust fund money to cover up a settlement error. Betty told Leo, and they decided to blackmail Daphne." Daphne hung her head. I took a sip of my wine this time and continued.

"Leo needed a place to hide while Daphne got the money, as he knew that Fat Saul was looking for him. Daphne told him about the Park View Terrace construction site. When I told her that it was Fat Saul who was after Leo, she made a phone call letting him know of Leo's whereabouts. You know what happened next. Fat Saul ended up dead. When Daphne learned of Betty's other identity, that of Lizzy Marks, she tracked her down. By Daphne's own admission, she paid her a visit and they went at it hammer and tongs."

Olive let out a high-pitched laugh. "They went at it like a couple of Jersey whores, is what they did," she said with a grin.

Daphne and Max regarded Olive with wide-eyed concern.

"Olive?" Max whispered. "What's gotten into you? Are you all right?"

Olive waved away his concern. "I'm fine. Don't mind me."

I continued. "Now, Daphne says that Betty/Lizzy was alive when she left her apartment, and I believe her. I think that when she left, she was seen by Leo, who then assumed that he'd been double crossed. I believe that he attacked Lizzy and killed her. When Audrey went to the apartment, she found Leo's cufflink in the dead woman's hand, and Leo later admitted to her that he had killed Lizzy."

Olive let out an annoyed sigh. "Nicole. We already know all this. Why are you rehashing it now?"

"Because I'm trying to create the timeline leading up to Leo's death," I explained. "As you know, Leo came home to Audrey in time for her party, but first he collected his money from Daphne. He had her pay off his debt and then went out to celebrate. Of course, we all know what happened then. He made a rather splashy spectacle of himself at a strip club that ended up in several newspapers."

Olive sniffed in disgust. "The man was a pig on all levels. The embarrassment he brought to this family was intolerable."

"I quite agree," I said. "However, when he finally did return home to Audrey, he was in for a surprise. Audrey had had enough.

She wanted a divorce. Leo knew that due to the pre-nup he'd be left with nothing. So he did what he always did when his back was up against the wall. He got nasty. He told her that if she tried to divorce him he'd say she'd killed Lizzy in a jealous rage. Then he called Daphne and put the screws to her, telling her that unless she paid him even more, he'd reveal that he'd seen her leaving Lizzy's apartment."

Daphne put her face in her hands. "Why do we have to go over this again?"

"Hang on, I'm getting there. By the night of Audrey's party, Leo had managed to enrage just about everyone in this family."

"Well, that's not *their* fault," interjected Toby.

"I didn't say it was, Toby. And, just so we're clear, I include *you* in that group."

Toby blinked twice before replying. "Me? What reason would I have to kill Leo? I didn't like that man, I'll admit, but that doesn't mean I would kill him."

"I would respectfully disagree with that assessment, Toby," I said. "I think you'd do just about anything for Audrey. Especially if that anything meant that you got a second chance with her."

Toby bristled. "Now see here, I don't like what you're saying."

"Neither do I, Toby. But, it's true. You wanted Leo dead as much as anyone else at this table. Why don't you tell me what happened? Was it a spur-of-the-moment decision? You were visibly upset at his returning to Audrey. Had you had enough and just snapped, or had you planned it all along?"

Toby began to sputter. "Now, wait a minute!"

I cut him off. "What happened? What made you decide to follow Leo into the men's room and kill him?"

"Stop this!" cried Audrey. "Toby didn't stab Leo."

I looked at her. "And how do you know that?"

She took a gulp of air before answering. "Because I did."

FORTY-FOUR

"*Audrey!*" exclaimed Olive. "What are you saying?"

"The truth," I answered.

Audrey looked at me in bewilderment. "Wait. You already knew? Then why did you say Toby did it?"

I shrugged. "I figured if you heard Toby accused of stabbing Leo, you'd be forced to speak up."

Audrey propped her elbows on the table on sank her head in her hands. "I've been such an idiot."

"Well, yes," I admitted. "But you didn't kill him. At least you have that."

"Wait," said Toby, turning to Audrey. "So, you *did* stab Leo?"

A half sob escaped Audrey's mouth. "I couldn't take it anymore. I told him that I was done. That it was over." She pulled her hands away from her face and looked at me. "I told you how he laughed at me. He told me that if I tried to divorce him, he'd not only try to destroy me, but Daphne as well. I couldn't let him do that. During the party, I saw him go into the bathroom. I waited until I thought he was alone, and then I followed."

Toby interrupted her. "Wait, Audrey. Stop talking. As your lawyer, I insist that you don't say another word."

Audrey smiled fondly at him. "What's the point, Toby? She already knows. Besides, it's the truth."

"Yes, but …" continued Toby.

Audrey spoke over him. "Please, Toby. Let me finish. I'm tired of pretending." She turned back to me. "Where was I?"

"You followed Leo into the bathroom," I prompted.

"Oh, yes," she said. "I followed him in there. I was in a kind of cold rage. It was almost as if I was watching myself rather than actually doing it."

"Do you hear that?" said Toby. "She was having an out-of-body experience. By her own admission, she was in a dream state."

No one paid attention to him. Audrey continued, "He was sitting in the chair. His back was to me. I can't remember if I said anything. I just … stabbed him. Then I walked out." She shot me a rueful glance. "And then I started screaming. You know the rest."

Toby grabbed her hand and held it tight. Audrey sat back in her chair. "So, now what?"

"Well, I'm not sure," I said turning to Max. "What is the charge for stabbing a dead body?"

"I'm a bit rusty on that one myself," he admitted. "Desecration?"

"Sounds about right," I agreed. "In any case, it's better than murder. Lucky for you, someone else got to him first."

"This is absurd!" snapped Olive. "I refuse to sit here and listen to any more of this nonsense!"

"Well, I think you should," I said. "It's about to get interesting."

Olive's eyes narrowed. "What are you talking about?"

"I'm talking about who killed Leo," I replied. "Audrey stabbed him, but as we all know, someone poisoned him. It was the poison that killed him."

"That could have been anyone," Olive snapped. "It probably was one of those men who were after Leo before. The ones he owed money to."

"Well, it is interesting that you bring that up. I don't know if you remember, but one of your guests, Janet Harris, mentioned something about a rude waiter. She also mentioned that he had a tattoo. I didn't think much of it at the time, but later I wondered about it. There is a man who works for Frank Little who has a very distinctive tattoo. So, I called Janet Harris and asked her to describe the tattoo, which she very kindly did."

"And?" said Max. "What did she say?"

"The tattoo she described matches the one belonging to the gentleman in question," I answered.

"Gentleman might be a bit of an exaggeration," said Nigel.

"Duly noted," I replied.

Max frowned. "Does this tattooed man have a name?"

"Yes, he does. I think of him as Talons. However, that's not his legal name. His real name is Marvin Gibbs."

"Get out of here!" exclaimed Nigel.

I raised my hand. "Hand to God."

Nigel shook his head. "Well, he'll always be Talons to me."

Max leaned forward. "So, this man ... Marvin?"

"Let's just stick with Talons," I said. "It's easier."

Max nodded. "So, this man, Talons, he killed Leo?"

"Yes," I answered. "Well, technically."

Max's eyes narrowed. "What do you mean *technically*?"

"Well, I mean technically in the sense that he delivered the fatal drink to Leo," I said.

Everyone began to talk at once. "Who is he?" "How?" "Where is he now?"

I raised my hand to stop the questions. "To answer in the order received. He was a member of Frank Little's crew. He donned a waiter's uniform and blended in with the other wait staff at Audrey's birthday party. He's now in police custody."

"So, why did he kill Leo? Did Leo owe him money too?" asked Daphne.

I took a sip of wine. "Well, that's where it gets tricky," I admitted.

"Why?" asked Daphne. "Why would it get tricky?"

I took another sip of my wine before answering. "Because he claims he didn't supply the poison. He says someone else supplied it. Along with the waiter's jacket."

Max frowned. "Who?"

I took a deep breath. "Olive," I said.

FORTY-FIVE

THERE WERE SEVERAL GASPS. Max cursed. Olive stayed very still. She stared back at me almost defiantly. Then she laughed. It had a high-pitched ring to it. "That's absurd," she said. "Why would I want to kill Leo?"

"Because he was a public embarrassment to this family. Because he was slowly destroying Audrey. Because he was blackmailing your daughter."

Olive reached for her purse and took out another pill. She washed it down with a gulp of her gin and tonic. "Mother!" said Daphne. "You can't take those with alcohol!"

Olive ignored her. Staring at me, she said, "You've gone too far, Nicole. I can't believe you would tell such a horrible lie." Max pushed back his chair and stood up. He walked over to Olive and put a reassuring hand on her shoulder.

"I assume that this bizarre accusation comes from this man Talons?" asked Max.

I nodded. "It does."

"Well, I hardly think that that will stand up in court as evidence," he scoffed. "I don't know why this man chose to poison Leo, but I think it's obvious that once he was caught, he tried to shift the blame on Olive."

"I wish it was only that, Max," I said. "But, it's not."

Max looked uneasily from Olive to me. "I'm sorry, Max. I really am," I said. "But Olive can't walk away from this." I signaled Danny. He got up from his seat at the bar and went into the back office. Moments later he returned with Frank. Upon seeing him, Olive blanched. Danny and Frank walked over to our table. I stood up. "Everyone, this is Frank Little," I said. "Frank, I believe you know most everyone here. Now would you care to repeat what you told me earlier?"

Frank nodded. "Sure thing. The other day, this lady here," Frank pointed at Olive, "came here and offered me money to help her get rid of Leo."

"That's a lie!" Olive shouted at Frank. Max kept his hand on her shoulder. It now restrained her rather than comforted her.

Frank ignored her. "I told her no. I told her that I wasn't interested in that kind of work. But Talons followed her outside. He wasn't particular like me."

"My client, Mr. Little, is a scrupulous businessman," interjected Flynn. "I want that noted."

Nigel made a sort of coughing noise. So, too, did his father. "Yes, Mr. Flynn," said Paul with a small smile. "We'll all agree that Mr. Little is the epitome of conscientiousness."

Frank glanced suspiciously at Nigel and Paul. "Yeah, well I don't know about that. But I do know that Talons agreed to do the job for her. He told me. I told him it was a bad idea, but Talons ain't too bright."

"Mr. Gibb's level of intelligence will, of course, be a major factor in our defense," said Flynn. "He was obviously unduly influenced by a woman of superior intellect and education. I plan on proving that Mr. Gibbs was used as a pawn in …"

"Save it for the judge, Flynn," I said.

"This is absurd!" yelled Olive. Her voice was getting thicker. Her words were starting to slur. "Are you seriously taking the word of this … this Neanderthal? Why, it's insulting! It's ludicrous!"

"Unfortunately it's also true, Olive," I said, my tone gentle. "You wanted Leo gone. You couldn't stand what he had done to Audrey. She'd changed, and you were desperate. Then, somehow, you found out how he was blackmailing Daphne. By the time the papers splattered pictures of the kind of man Leo was for all of New York to see, his fate was sealed. You had decided to take matters into your own hands. You were going to make sure Leo Blackwell never hurt this family again."

For a brief second, an expression of keen lucidity flashed across Olive's face. Her eyes locked on mine with an intense gaze. "Prove it!" she snapped. A second later, the expression was replaced with one of confusion. Her face began to crumple. Audrey got up from her chair and slowly walked over to Olive. Kneeling by her chair, Audrey said, "Aunt Olive? Is this true? Did you do this?"

Olive placed her hand on Audrey's cheek. Her eyes welled with tears. "Oh, Audrey," she said, her voice a choked whisper. "You're so beautiful. So much like your father. He was my baby brother. I loved him so much. And when he and your mother died, a part of me died, too. But, I swore to him … to his memory … that I would never let any harm come to you." She turned to Paul and Doris, her eyes pleading for understanding. "You understand, don't you, Paul? It's family. We were raised to stick by each other. Daddy always said that we had an obligation to protect the family."

Paul regarded Olive with a pained expression. Beside him, Doris grabbed his hand tightly. She nodded at Olive. "We understand, Olive," she said quietly.

Olive sank back a little in her chair. She turned to Audrey. "He was coming to me in my dreams, you know," she said softly. "Your father. He told me that he wanted Leo gone." She looked up at Max. "Remember, Max? I told you about those dreams." Max nodded, his face etched in misery. Olive didn't appear to notice. She turned back to Audrey. "You are like a second daughter to me, Audrey. I love you."

Audrey remained kneeling. She, too, began to cry. "Oh, Aunt Olive," she moaned.

Olive stroked her face gently. "But now you're okay. Leo is gone. I made sure of that. I can rest now. I can tell your father that you are safe." She took another sip of her drink. She seemed to have slipped into another world. She sat calmly; an eerily serene smile on her face. Looking up at Max, she said, "I think I need to lie down, Max. I feel so sleepy."

Max's face was a portrait of pain. He forced a smile on his face and nodded. "Of course, dear. Let's get you out of here."

FORTY-SIX

Max gently helped Olive to her feet. "Where are we going, Max?" Olive asked, her voice sleepy.

"We're going to get you well," he said. "Daphne, I will call you when I get her settled." He threw a challenging look at me. I gave a nod of my head indicating that he could take Olive. Max gave me a brief nod of thanks before gently escorting Olive out of the restaurant.

Once they left, we all sat there in silence. "Where is he taking her?" asked Doris.

"To the nearest hospital or treatment center, I would imagine," answered Daphne. "She's bonkers! Those pills have made her go bonkers."

"Exactly!" said Toby, jumping on the explanation. "That's exactly what our defense will be. She is clearly addled from the pills and is not in control of her faculties. She needs treatment, not judgment."

Nigel looked at me questioningly. I shrugged. I'd seen worse defense arguments succeed. After a three-month stint at a plushy rehab spa—one with a calming ocean view, of course—Olive would be deemed rehabilitated. Her attending doctor would then no doubt claim that Olive's actions were the result of the drugs and not her own rational thinking. Given Leo's own morally repugnant nature and the likelihood of his own murderous actions, it was unlikely that Olive would face anything more than continued drug rehab and a monitored probation. And based on what Toby was saying, he and Max would throw up enough legal road blocks that would ensure that Olive never saw the inside of a jail. It was one of those truths that people hate to admit, but money buys freedom. And God knows the Martini family had that.

I needed to call Marcy, and I was going to. However, I decided to postpone that phone call until I knew that Olive had been admitted to whatever facility Max was taking her. For some reason, I felt I owed Olive that.

Flynn got up from his bar seat and walked over to me. Reaching into his suit pocket, he pulled out one of his cards. "In my professional opinion, I think your aunt has an excellent chance for an acquittal. Clearly, she was in some kind of fugue state. If you would be so kind to pass along my card, I'd be happy to provide her with a consultation—free of charge, of course."

I smiled and took the card. "I'll make sure this ends up in the appropriate hands." He afforded me an oily smile and returned to his seat at the bar.

I took a sip of my drink. It wasn't all too bad, really. In a way I'd miss Olive when she was doped up on Valium. It was the only time that she ever called me Nic.

———

It was late by the time Nigel and I returned to the hotel. After Max took Olive to wherever she'd be spending the next several months, the rest of us stayed at Little's Vittles. Audrey quietly wept in her seat while Toby tried to comfort her. Daphne then pulled her chair up next to her. Pulling her close, they had a long, private conversation. Whatever Daphne said made an impact on Audrey. She seemed to perk up after their chat, much to the apparent relief of Toby. The two of them held hands for the rest of the evening.

After that we had a surprisingly good time, despite the food. Frank might not know cuisine, but the man knew how to stock a bar. It was after one when we left. It seemed the right time to leave, as Nigel had begun to instruct the bartender on the proper way to shake a martini. He claimed that the trick was to shake the canister to the beat of Glenn Miller's "In the Mood". When we finally filed out to our waiting limo, Frank, Danny, and the bartender were all taking turns shaking it to the beat.

FORTY-SEVEN

I AWOKE THE NEXT morning to a large pair of honey-brown eyes gazing into mine. "Nigel?"

"Yes?"

"Why is Skippy in our bed?" I reached over to the head belonging to the brown eyes and scratched it. Skippy thumped his tail happily.

"He pushed me out about an hour ago," Nigel answered from the breakfast table.

"You give up awfully easy," I said. I sat up, stretched my arms over my head, and yawned. "What time is it?"

Nigel looked at his watch. "Ten-thirty. I had breakfast sent up," he said. He took a sip of what looked like a Bloody Mary. "They sent up some coffee with it, too," he added with a mystified glance at the silver pot, "although I can't imagine why. Would you like some?"

I laughed. "Yes, please."

Nigel poured me a cup and brought it over. Before handing it to me, he bent down and kissed me. "First course," he explained before handing me the cup.

"You'll never top it," I said and took a sip.

He shoved Skippy over and sat on the edge of the bed. "How are you this morning?"

"Fine. How are *you*?"

"I always said half of my family probably should be in jail. I guess it's a start."

I scoffed. "You know as well as I do that Aunt Olive isn't going to do any jail time. Toby, Daphne, and Max will see to that."

Nigel opened his eyes wide in amusement. "Hey! You just called her Aunt Olive!"

"So I did," I admitted. "I guess she suddenly seems more like family to me now. After all, while you think most of your family should be in jail, most of mine actually *were*. At least at one point or another."

Nigel laughed and kissed me again. "Just one of the many reasons I love you, Mrs. Martini. You help wash away my air of respectability."

I kissed him back. "Speaking of which, what are your plans for today?" I asked.

"I don't know. What did you have in mind?"

"Well, I believe we are supposed to fly home tonight," I said.

"You want to postpone that?"

"No, but I believe you are forgetting someone, dear." I looked at Skippy. He thumped his tail. "I don't think he counts as carry on."

"Yes, but apparently he counts as a *medical* dog."

I sighed. "I don't want to know, do I?"

He considered my question. "Probably not," he admitted. "In fact, the more confused you appear about the whole situation, the better it will be."

I laughed again and pulled him close. "Deal. Now, until then, why don't we work on your pesky problem of respectability?"

Skippy let out a protesting bark, but he did get off the bed.

Skippy: 2,468; Us: 1.

ABOUT THE AUTHOR

Tracy Kiely received a BA in English from Trinity College. This accomplishment prompted most job interviewers to ask, "How fast can you type?" Her standard answer of "not so fast" usually put an end to further questions.

She was eventually hired by the American Urological Association (AUA), who were kind enough to overlook the whole typing thing—mainly because they knew just what kind of prose she'd be typing. After several years, Tracy left the AUA, taking with her a trove of anecdotal stories that could eventually result in her banishment from polite society. That's when she thought writing a novel might be a good idea.

Murder with a Twist is her first novel in the Nic and Nigel Martini series. It can be enjoyed straight up or with a twist. She is also the author of the Jane Austen-inspired Elizabeth Parker mystery series: *Murder at Longbourn*, *Murder on the Bride's Side*, *Murder Most Persuasive*, and *Murder Most Austen*. These can be enjoyed with either tea or a very dry sherry.

Tracy lives in Maryland with her husband and three children.